The Lives of Kelvin Fletcher

Miller Williams

The Lives of Kelvin Fletcher

STORIES MOSTLY SHORT

The University of Georgia Press   *Athens & London*

Published by the University of Georgia Press
Athens, Georgia 30602
© 2002 by Miller Williams
All rights reserved
Set in 10 on 14 New Caledonia by Bookcomp, Inc.
Printed and bound by Maple-Vail
The paper in this book meets the guidelines for
permanence and durability of the Committee on
Production Guidelines for Book Longevity of the
Council on Library Resources.

Printed in the United States of America
06 05 04 03 02 C 5 4 3 2 1

Library of Congress Cataloging-in-Publication Data

Williams, Miller.
   The lives of Kelvin Fletcher : stories mostly
short / Miller Williams.
      p. cm.
   ISBN 0-8203-2439-6 (hardcover : alk. paper)
   1. Arkansas—Social life and customs—Fiction.
2. Young men—Fiction.   3. Boys—Fiction.
I. Title.
PS3545.I53352 L57 2002
813'.54—dc21   2002001550

British Library Cataloging-in-Publication Data available

For Jordan

and

in memory of
John William Corrington
co-conspirator

Every story is about someone who wants something while someone or something stands for a while or forever in the way. These are about one Kelvin Fletcher, sometime around the middle of the twentieth century, who wanted to be good and wanted to grow up. What stood in the way of either was the other.

Happiness isn't something you experience;
it's something you remember.

OSCAR LEVANT

CONTENTS

The Lives of Kelvin Fletcher

One Saturday Afternoon

Kelvin Fletcher let the door of the Rex Theater swish heavily shut behind him. He squinted his eyes against the sudden daylight and felt the heat rush up and over him. He was conscious of the concrete and the cars, the bicycles parked in a crazy huddle, and the Saturday shoppers, mostly country people and colored folks. He waited for the others to come out so they could look together at the stills framed outside the theater, alongside the poster announcing the movie: Johnny Mack Brown in *Desperate Trails*. The serial was *Scouts to the Rescue* with Jackie Cooper. It was the first chapter. Last week was the last chapter of *The Lone Ranger,* and Kelvin was pretty sure *Scouts to the Rescue* wasn't going to measure up to it. Probably there wasn't a serial as good as *The Lone Ranger* except *The Shadow* or maybe *The Green Hornet*.

They were pointing out the stills, one by one.

"They showed that!"

"Yeah. But they didn't show *that*." Ralph rammed his index finger into Johnny Mack Brown's face and then put it back into his nose.

"How come they leave things out?"

The examining of the stills was a means of reentry into the bright world, a ritualistic depressurizing period that made it possible to move from in there to out here. It only took three or four minutes but it was important. It had to be done. No one would any more have walked past the pictures without checking them against the truth on the screen than he would have walked down Chickasaw Avenue to get past the concrete and into the residential section. The five-block trip from the movie to the first vacant lot was made, of course, through the alley that led behind Rackley's Department Store and Kress's. Sometimes there were things thrown away no one would believe. Kelvin had not seen but he had heard of pocket knives and watches, still in their boxes, being found in the trash from the stores. He believed the stories, but although he hunted every week through the enormous trash bins, sometimes losing himself in the boxes and paper, he secretly hoped he would never find such a thing. He knew it would have been thrown out by mistake, and so he would have to give it back. And that would be, he felt pretty sure, the end of the gang.

There were four of them and they were ten.

Ralph was almost ten. He was fat and couldn't run fast but you were done for if he ever caught you. Joe Bob's father was dead, and he lived with his mother out past the cottonseed oil mill where the bus turned around. L. W. was usually the leader because he was the tallest and the strongest except for Ralph and mostly because he lived in the fire station. His father was the man who cranked the alarm on top of the station to call the volunteers from their stores and offices, and L. W. turned it once by himself. He said, anyway, that he had. Ralph said, "You ain't never!" but Kelvin believed it. He believed anything that ought to be true if you couldn't prove it wasn't. It had come to him suddenly one Saturday morning when he was sitting on the commode wondering how it feels to be a girl that it felt however he imagined it did. Because if you can't know what something is for sure, and those who know can't tell you, anything you decide to believe is as true as anything else. The world was in two parts. Things you can know about and things you can't guess. It's the things you can't know that you can do with what you want to. This was a great revelation to Kelvin. As if he had found a kit he could make worlds with. It was his God kit, and he would sometimes lie for hours on the roof of his father's carport or atop the great pile of hulls behind the cotton gin and compose worlds, playing with unknowable things, in the glorious knowledge that they had all the qualities you gave them. He ordered worlds with winds that give milk and trees that dream. Worlds of crows that are words in disguise and houses that remember what happens in them. He decided this was how God made up the world to start with. He wondered what would happen to the world when God stopped thinking about it.

Always, on the way home from the movie, it was the same game, always an argument.

"You can be Buck Jones," L. W. said, "I'm Bob Steele."

"You were Bob Steele last time," Ralph said. "Be Wild Bill Hickok. What's wrong with Wild Bill Hickok?"

"Ain't nothing wrong with him. That's who Kelvin's bein'. Jesus' name, Ralph. You act more like Gabby Hayes."

"Why don't you be Clyde Beatty?" Joe Bob said, and the other three boys laughed until he laughed with them, not sure what was funny.

"Clyde Beatty ain't no cowboy, Joe Bob," Kelvin cried, swinging himself under the gray wire of a telephone pole. "He's a lion tamer!"

"I don't care. I got to go home anyways. I'll see you all at Sunday school maybe," and Joe Bob slipped from the alley, skittering like a cat between the brick buildings in the direction of his home.

"You can be Wild Bill Hickok," Kelvin said to L. W. "I gotta go too, anyway. If I don't cut the grass this afternoon, I'm gonna git it."

"How can we play with two people?" L. W. said, "You don't have to go."

"Yes, I do. My dad got a belt." Before Kelvin had three words out, L. W. was crawling over the low wooden wall of a trash bin, Ralph puffing to get his bulk over ahead of him. Kelvin took off at a fast run to clear the wall with a clumsy jump and a high wobbling scream. He landed on a large box that said Rexall in red letters and felt it flatten under him. Then L. W. landed on top of him and then Ralph, calling "Dog pile! Dog pile!" For a long time, until all three of them were hot and filthy, they wrestled in the pile of boxes, playing King of the Mountain with a mountain that collapsed underneath the king and swallowed him up.

Until finally Ralph and L. W. were gone, and Kelvin climbed, sweating and breathing hard, over the once-painted wall. Straddling it, he would barely touch his tiptoes to the pavement of the alley. "Giddy up," he cried, "giddy up," and the green stallion snorted and reared back, twisted and bucked, beating the earth hard and raising great clouds of red dust.

Kelvin fought the creature with all the will and courage of Wild Bill Hickok until he got a splinter in his hand, and then he got off.

He was about to leave the alley and make his way across Fifth Street to the alley in the next block when he heard the *shuf-shuf* sound that he loved more than all the other sounds of the streets. His dull blue eyes brightened. He looked toward Chickasaw Avenue, and sure enough there he was, moving very slowly, putting his feet down as if he was putting them into house slippers—*shuf* and *shuf* and *shuf*.

Blind Jubie Hawkins was making his way slowly down the street, his white hair kinked tight against his skull, his eyes, like blobs of clabber milk, half-filling the deep holes in his head. His head was erect, jerking a little with each abrupt step, and his fingers moved easily over the strings of an old guitar. With each jerk of his head there was a tinkle of metal on metal from the tin cup tied with a shoestring to the head of Blind Jubie's git-fiddle. Kelvin stood still until the old Negro had passed him, and then he fell in behind him, walking quietly and waiting.

He didn't have to wait so long at the next corner. The steady strumming modulated and picked up spirit, and Kelvin knew what was coming. He closed his eyes a few seconds and joined Blind Jubie in a holy darkness until the weary ghost-ridden voice rose over the tinny rhythm of the strings and lifted Kelvin up into the gathering clouds.

Hey God, God don't ever change
Hey God, God don't ever change

At the corner they turned left and a woman dropped some kind of coin in the cup. Blind Jubie said "God bless you" without breaking his rhythm.

Well—God in—creation
God when Adam fell
He's God way up in Heaven
He's God way down in Hell

Kelvin felt in his pocket for a nickel, and from far off a long roll of thunder blurred Blind Jubie's words. Kelvin moved up closer to him and moved his lips to the lines.

God in the pulpit
God without at the door
He's God in every corner
He's God all over the floor

The black man stopped his feet and guitar and voice all together so that Kelvin almost ran into him. A drop of rain fell.

"Hello, boy," Blind Jubie said without turning around or lifting his hands from the silent strings.

"Hi, Brother Jubie." He dropped his nickel into the tin cup.

"Did you go to the show?"

"Yes."

"Did you see God in it?"

"I don't rightly know."

"If you can't see God in it you ought not go. Ain't that what we decided?"

"This is Saturday, Brother Jubie. You said Sunday's God's day."

The long crooked finger began to splay over the strings again and fell into a slow, heavy beat. A few large separate drops of rain splattered on the sidewalk.

"I never said that, boy. Ain't nothin' not God's. They's some things he lets people use. But people ain't got nothin'. Not one day in the week nor a mouthful of tobacco nor a penny in a potful. Nor no son nor no daughter. And you ain't got a ma or paw God ain't lettin' you use. Ain't that what I told you?"

Kelvin was still standing behind the preacher, looking at the place on his back where the clothesline holding the guitar ran from his shoulder across the faded work shirt down to the other side.

"Yessir."

Suddenly the *shuf-shuf* began again and the music came louder. A man dropped in a coin.

"God bless you." And in a low voice without feeling, "Don't say sir to me, boy. You gonna have enough troubles."

My Lord, what a mourning
My Lord, what a mourning
My Lord, what a mourning
When the skies begin to fall

The rain was a steady whisper now, and a faint layer of steam began to rise from the street. Kelvin took a couple of steps to follow Blind Jubie and then he stopped because he was heading away from his home where the grass was already too wet to cut. He stood for most of a minute while his shirt was slowly soaked and the music was drowned. Finally he saw Blind Jubie stop under a canvas awning and take out his handkerchief to wipe the water off his guitar, then off his forehead and his deep gullied face. Then Blind Jubie ran the handkerchief back over the briar patch of his head and crammed it back into his hip pocket. Kelvin was satisfied. He turned around and stepped into an easy lope toward home. His shirt glued now to his back and his tennis shoes splatting on the wet pavement, he ran past the Gulf station and the taxi stand and into the alley behind Cook's Cleaners.

He stopped as he did every Saturday before the steam pipe that ran out of the back wall of the cleaners only a couple of inches from the ground, the long, vicious rod like a shotgun barrel that every few seconds hissed a boiling cloud from somewhere inside the cleaners out to the alley behind, testing the guts of anyone brave enough to stand in front of it. It was low, not more than four inches off the ground, so that the silver-white cloud rolled first with violent contortions along the blacktop of the valley and then lifted slowly, spreading out of shape but still hot, until it disappeared into nothing overhead and became a part of the sky. Kelvin rolled his blue jeans to his knees and took his position in front of the pipe, waiting for the next blast. He ground his teeth together and clenched his fists, determined not to jump away. This time he would hold his ground. He would stand still. He waited in the rain with his eyes closed and his hands over his ears so that he wouldn't be warned by the noise or the first slow steam spilling ahead of the blast, and he started to sing.

> I will not be, I will not be moved
> I will not be, I will not be moved
> just like a tree . . .

He jumped two feet, as if he were being suddenly jerked up into heaven, somersaulted off to his right and rolled under a low shed where garbage from the Red Dot Cafe was stashed in boxes and rusty buckets, ready for the farmers to collect for their pigs. He stuck his hand into a cantaloupe rind and let out some sound of disgust. He started to jump to his feet and hit his head on the low roof. He fell down and wrapped his arms around the back of his head. He began to cry.

When he stopped crying and opened his eyes it wasn't raining. He was still lying in a heap under the shed roof and thought to get up slowly. He rubbed his eyes with the balls of his hands and tried to focus. They focused on a wiggling mass of small pink creatures, jerking their feet and countless heads, squeaking and going nowhere, trying desperately to crawl somewhere on the asphalt, not six inches in front of his face.

"Puppies!" he said out loud. "A new litter of puppies!" He reached out and let his fingertips touch them. There was no hair, and he saw that their eyes were not open. He worked his finger under the belly of one of the largest, smaller than his thumb, and let it roll in two clumsy flops into his palm. It was warm and soft with new life. Kelvin made a deep bed of his hand and moved carefully out from under the shed roof to find a box of the right size. In five minutes he was on his way home with his secret cargo in a grease-blackened box that said Delco Rings.

He walked past the church without looking up. In the vacant lot three boys who knew his name were spinning tops on the damp but hard-packed path cutting through the lot. They looked at Kelvin a second and decided he didn't have anything they wanted and went on spinning their tops.

"Just what would you all think," Kelvin said almost out loud, "if you looked in this box with the Delco Rings and there was seven new puppies?" He narrowed his eyes and smiled like a spy and took to the alleys again until he was home.

He let the screen door to the back porch slam shut and flew into the kitchen to show his mother. "Look what I found," he said, panting and full of himself. He sat the box gently on the checked oil cloth of the kitchen table where the dishes for supper were already in place, ready for the cornbread and probably sweet potatoes Kelvin had smelled as he came through the backyard, and for Mr. Fletcher, who was not yet home.

"Don't you put that greasy thing down in here, Kelvin. It's got grease all over it!"

He picked it up and put it on the floor, squatting over it so that it lay between his knees. He turned it around in his hands a couple of times, waiting for the next reaction from his mother. She sniffed the way she always did when she was tired, and pushed a sweep of sweaty brown hair away from her eyes with the back of her hand, and then she looked down at him.

"What is it, Kelvin?"

"In this box is seven brand new puppies. They ain't even got their eyes open yet." Saying this he snapped the flaps of the box back and presented his marvelous pink tumbling high-voiced children to his mother.

"Merciful God, Kelvin!" Mrs. Fletcher said. "You've brought home a whole litter of rats."

Kelvin had never heard his mother swear before and the oath echoed in his ears as he looked down in disbelief at the little dogs that had all at once become rodents. He looked up at his mother, his mouth trying to say something, his eyes swelling with surprise and disappointment.

"They're not dogs?"

"Where ever in the world did you get hold of those things?"

"They're not dogs?"

"No, they're not dogs, Kelvin. Where did they come from?"

"Out behind the Red Dot Cafe. They were by their selves. The mother had gone off."

"There wasn't any mother. Those are rats, Kelvin. The mother had most likely been killed already and someone come across her litter and threw it out. Now, you get rid of it and clean up for supper." The order given, Mrs. Fletcher turned her attention finally away from Kelvin and back for a moment to the stove. She closed the oven door and stood up. "Go on now, Kelvin. You're daddy's going to be home in a few minutes. He won't like those things in the kitchen."

Kelvin interlocked the flaps and still squatting lifted the sealed box to his chest, grasping it between his spread palms.

"What you aim for me to do with them? Can't I keep them in the smokehouse?"

"We already got rats out there. We don't need any more." Mrs. Fletcher bent again to the oven, and this time the cornbread was done and she took it out. She set the pan on the top of the stove. "Take them down in the basement and drown them."

Kelvin felt a chunk of ice fall into his stomach. He wanted to get up but he couldn't. He put the box down on the linoleum and squatted beside it.

"How come I got to drown them?"

"Because you brought them into the house, Kelvin. Who would you expect to do it?"

"How come anybody's got to do it?"

"Because."

"Because *why*?"

"Because they're rats!"

After supper, when his father was reading the paper in the living room and listening to the radio, Kelvin went down to the basement. He could just barely hear the sounds of a news program, that bombs fell on London last night, until his mother, passing through the hall, closed the cellar door. Then there was silence. Kelvin opened the box on the crude wooden water-stained table his mother washed clothes on and looked at the little rats as if he still thought they might be dogs. Finally he turned to the wall behind him, took a zinc tub off a nail and set it gently on the floor. He leaned over the box, resting on his elbows, and stared into it, thinking what to do next. He didn't like the idea of drowning them and he thought of smashing them with a brick. But it would have to be done one at a time, and he knew he would never make it all the way through seven. He found the hose his mother used on washdays and put the end of it in the tub and turned on the water. It made a high rattly sound. Kelvin sat on the bottom step of the stairs to hear the sound change like a slow trombone until the water swallowed up the end of the hose and again there was silence, except for the barely audible scratching inside the box.

The radio reached down into the basement again, and Mrs. Fletcher followed its sound down the stairs. She stood above Kelvin. He didn't look up at her but he could see her black shoes with both the laces broken and knotted. In the living room his father was listening to something about Joe Louis.

"Use a mason jar, Kelvin. Fill it up and put a lid on it. It's quicker."

Kelvin went to the wall faucet and turned off the water. He kept his hand on the valve and his eyes too, away from his mother.

"Why can't I put them back?"

"You mean, where you found them?"

Kelvin nodded.

Mrs. Fletcher turned to go back up the steps. She stood with her right hand on the two-by-four railing and the fingers of her left hand pushed against the bridge of her nose as if it was about to fall off her face and she was trying to mold it back on.

"They'd starve to death, Kelvin. This is the best thing you can do for them."

Kelvin heard her shoes on the wooden steps and heard the cellar door shut. He didn't hear the radio anymore.

He filled a quart jar from the half-filled tub and coldly lifted one of the animals from the box and dropped it in. There was a small plop and splash and he watched as the tiny rat sank to the bottom and floated to the top, then sank again and began to rise. Quickly he emptied the jar back into the tub, holding his hand loosely over the mouth of the jar to keep the rat from going out. When it fell against his fingers he knew that it was still alive. He jerked away when it wiggled against his palm and fell into the tub.

"God!" he said, plunging his hands into the cold clear water. Three times when he closed them on the elusive figure it swirled up between his thumbs and down to the bulls-eye bottom of the tub, caught in the tumbling currents Kelvin made as he sloshed about wildly. When he caught it on the fourth try, the rat was dead, soft and soppy wet in his fingers. He saw for the first time that there was a light down over the body that now, wet and pasted to the flesh, made the rat look like another animal, as if it had drowned as one thing and come up from the water as something else. A shiver ran across Kelvin's shoulders but he knew he wasn't going to cry. He dropped the dead rat into the empty jar and one by one let its six brothers slide down the side of the jar into a writhing pile at the bottom. With the hose he filled the jar, watching the animals swish and flip in the maelstrom until the water was perfectly to the top, then he screwed on the lid. He set the jar on the table and set himself erect on his knees with his nose just at the jar and watched the drowning. Not because he wanted to. More than once he closed his eyes but he opened them quickly. His knees began to hurt but he couldn't move. For three or four minutes he watched what he had done. Six floated to the top and fell slowly to the bottom again and then four, fighting the water with their incredibly small arms. And then only two. They moved together for a long time, getting in each other's way and turning apart, rising and sinking together, then falling madly out of rhythm. Kelvin felt the rhythm of his own breathing. He felt himself under water, bumping his head against the metal lid, holding his breath, knowing the water could come into his lungs. Himself again, outside the jar, dry, he wanted to take the lid off, but he couldn't touch it. He was breathing hard, as if he had run a long way.

"Die!" he said. One of them did die, and lay quietly on the bottom. And then, a minute later, when his nose was so close to the jar he could feel the cold of it around his face, he watched the last red shape, still struggling instinctively upward, rub its blank face against the glass.

"Die!" Kelvin said, not sure anymore that he wouldn't cry. "Hurry up and die." And as he looked round-eyed in spite of himself he saw the left eye of the conscious thing pop open. His throat burst in one awful spasm and he cried out something unintelligible. That was all the crying he did. The last one stopped fighting and tumbled down to the bottom. It lay there on the others. Nothing moved.

For a moment he wanted to pray. But he had been God, and now the thought of God sickened him. He felt like he was going to vomit. He opened the mason jar and poured the water off and then put the lid back on. In the corner of the back yard a cat and a frog were buried, but this was not the place for these things.

He closed the cellar door behind him and walked down the hall and through the kitchen to the back porch. He heard voices of his mother and father in the living room. He couldn't tell what they were saying because the radio was blaring again about the bombs and London. He remembered the newsreel at the show. The screen was full of millions of Germans sticking their arms in the air saying "Seek hile, seek hile, seek hile!" But the rats had not been killed by bombs. He had drowned them. The only important thing now was to finish what he started.

Kelvin didn't recall leaving the house or passing the two graves in the yard, or crossing the street. He remembered turning down Fourth Street by the Holiness Church and passing Dr. Slaughter's office and knew that now he could see the stand of corn where Mr. Cardin's land started at the edge of town. He knew that not far beyond Cardin's farm was the river, where he was not ever to go alone. He knew that was where he was going.

He had meant to go around the farm, but when he got to the cornfield he bent under the barbed wire and walked straight through. His shoes sunk in the mud until they were heavy with ugly dull red blobs like the burlap Mr. Cardin put on his show horses' feet to make them step high. Kelvin stepped high as long as he could and then finally he couldn't pull his right foot out of the muck and he fell forward on his face, his arms over his head in front of him holding the jar. When he got up the cool wet clay hung onto him. He was transformed into something else, part boy, part earth, that neither his mother nor his father would have known.

In Mr. Cardin's yard, past the cornfield, the dogs didn't know him either. They barked at him, chasing him over a fence and down the river road. He didn't stop running until long after they had left off barking and been called back to the house by a curious and loud-voiced farmer who, Kelvin recalled, was storied to have shot at boys in his cornfield.

When Kelvin caught his breath he was passing the third farm-house. There was a light in a window. He looked into the woods on the other side of the road and saw that darkness was filling in between the trees. On the road it was still light, but dusk was falling. He walked faster. Beyond the next bend was the levee.

On the wet steep slope of the bank he fell again and slid halfway to the river. He dropped the jar and it rolled down with him. The mud was colder here. The river was swollen, and that always made him feel small and uneasy. Across the river, a few yards downstream, a couple of soldiers and a girl were sitting on an old pier. Kelvin could hear them laughing. He felt the cold working in toward his bones and began to shiver. His mouth twisted out of his control and tears came to his eyes.

Grandma, Grandma, let me in,
It's rainin' out here and I'm wet
to the skin.

He knew that what would happen to him because of the mud was not funny. And for going to the river anyway.

He hauled back and threw the jar as far as he could at the darkening water. It fell into the middle current and bobbed against the waves. The brass-colored top shone gold in the light of the low sun. Kelvin realized then he had forgotten to take off the lid and that the jar would float, maybe forever. He found a rock near his feet and with a loud grunt threw it at the jar. He missed. He threw another rock and missed again. He began to cry finally, a real saved-up blubbering cry, and kept throwing and crying as the jar floated every second further away. He picked up a handful of rocks and ran down closer to the water. Three times he slipped and fell down as the rock left his hand. He was crying now until he couldn't throw straight, and the jar was too far gone. Still he kept throwing toward it, knowing that he had failed the rats. That it was not finished. He knew that when you bring something home and drown it, then you're responsible.

Across the river, the soldiers and the girl were standing up, pointing toward the jar, almost in front of them now, turning red in the fading light, still catching the sun. Each of the soldiers in careful turn threw rocks at the jar while the girl squeaked delighted at the near misses. Kelvin let out a sound of anguish and frustration and shouted across the water.

"No! You don't do that! Don't you do it!" But there was no sign the soldiers heard him. They were looking around for some more rocks.

The girl had lost interest and began walking up the bank toward a Ford that was almost silhouetted against the twilight. The rumble seat and both doors were open. In the rumble seat someone was asleep. Kelvin called out again, and the wind opened its mouth and swallowed his words. The tall soldier gave up the hunt for rocks and followed after the girl. The other found something to throw and wound up like a baseball pitcher. He missed and yelled something to his companions that made them laugh and turn. Kelvin didn't say anything or move. The soldier threw again, and Kelvin knew as soon as the rock left his hand that this would be it. He heard the jar smash. In the rushing water of his mind he saw the small dogs, the rats, the rat terriers tumble free into the river. The tall soldier and the girl gave a cheer, and the victor, sharpshooter, ran up the bank to join them.

Kelvin walked home like the mummy in the movies, stiff, heavy-footed and covered with mud. He only said that he had been to the river. He took his whipping and took his bath and took a long time going to sleep.

The Year Ward West Took Away the Raccoon and Mr. Hanson's Garage Burned Down

Even though he did masturbate, Kelvin Fletcher went with his grandfather to church every Sunday somewhere in the four-county region around Booneville. He would hear his grandfather preach in the morning at one church and then in the evening at some other on the way home. If there wasn't dinner-on-the-ground, they would be invited to someone's home for fried chicken and dumplings, which was one of the good things about being a Methodist.

While they were moving along the highway, bad pavement and gravel, broken blacktop and gravel again, Kelvin would look through the hole in the floorboard where a screw had fallen out. He would see the road zooming underneath and always imagined he was on a flying carpet. Sitting beside him, his grandfather would tell about how it was when he was a boy, as skinny at ten as Kelvin.

There were stories about buggies and gunfights, and heavier snows and colder winters than Kelvin had known, and then Kelvin's great-grandfather, who fought in the War between the States and was captured by the Yankees and escaped out of the prison and went west to be a mule-skinner on the railroad. And how Kelvin's grandfather himself went for a while to Arizona in 1896 and saw a man get killed in front of a saloon by a preacher that wore guns.

Then Kelvin was holding on to his seat in a stage rumbling across the wooden bridges of Northern Virginia, the thin driver's face nothing but open mouth and eyes, his long arm popping the snake whip over the heads of the eight horses, brindle and black and bay. Then the stage turned into a gun wagon bouncing along the gullied roads of Arkansas to reinforce the outnumbered ranks of Captain Cordell at Pea Ridge. Then the gun wagon was a buckboard, flying across the flatlands of Arizona, Indians and Johnny Ringo and Pancho Villa close behind, shooting silver bullets. Then with a lurch the buckboard was a Dodge again, stopping for a pink-uddered cow standing broadside in the gravel. Kelvin's grandfather blew the horn, a long raw note like a rusty trumpet, and the old heifer lumbered across the ruts, braced her front legs against the soft earth, and, bottom high in the air, slid down into the ditch beside the road, disappeared, and popped up again on the far side. Kelvin was on his knees, watching her out of the back window as she grew smaller. *Little Boy Blue come blow your horn, the sheep are in the meadow and the cow is in the grass. There's a soldier in the grass with a bullet up his ass. Pull it out Uncle Sam pull it out.*

Kelvin turned to see if his grandfather had heard him, if he had spoken out loud, but the old man had not heard anything to disturb the awful surety with which he always sat behind the wheel, humming a hymn so softly Kelvin couldn't call the tune. The gray, wild bushes of his eyebrows made his eyes seem always to be in shadows and made the top of his face look stern, but his mouth was not stern at all. It seemed always about to grin.

His grandfather was right. It was not easy to be saved. Because when you are saved you know about being lost, but when you were lost you never thought about it. About going to hell. About how everybody has to line up in front of God and when it comes your turn he points to heaven or down where hell is and if you were lost the devil grabs hold of you.

"Will God go on forgiving you if you go on doing bad things?" Kelvin asked his grandfather one night as they were driving home from a late service in the next county.

"Over and over, Kelvin. Seventy times seven."

Kelvin calculated this to be 490. He figured he had probably sinned that much already. But if he just counted from the day when he was saved then he still had some to go.

"What happens when you use it all up?"

"That's a heap'a sin, Kelvin."

"But what would happen if you did?"

"Well then I guess you'd just sin yourself into the hot place."

Kelvin multiplied in his head again to be sure he hadn't made a mistake. It was 490.

In church he was safe. Kelvin never thought to pray for anything, but he listened to what his grandfather in the oaken pulpit prayed out of the boiling well of his mouth, the well of life.

It was only going home, after dark, lying in the back seat when his grandfather thought he was asleep, only then that he felt the guilt his heart held. He prayed God to forgive him for what God knew he did at night in bed and almost always in the bathtub, not to punish him anymore with the wet bed, the slick sticking pajamas, to forgive him for the bad words he said at school. And although he did not tell God, he had made up his mind, traveling these roads with his grandfather, listening to the hymns and watching his grandfather in the pulpits with the Bible in his hand, he had made up his mind to be a preacher.

"Cars a long time ago used to go 'Ah-oogah,' " he said when the cow had taken its tail with it into the corn.

"Kind of," his grandfather said, "But you got to suck when you say it, if you aim to sound like a T-model." His grandfather tightened his chest muscles and drew the red dust of the road through his mouth, open so the cheeks caved in, down through the voice box that Kelvin knew was full of iron bells and baling wire, and made a rusty cogwheel kind of "uh—oo—gah," and at that moment Kelvin was as proud of his grandfather as he had ever been. Then Kelvin tried it and it was pretty good. He laughed.

His grandfather took one dark, wrinkled hand from the wheel, which he didn't do very often, and put his arm around Kelvin. "The Lord loves you, Boy," he said, "and so do I."

"I love you, too," Kelvin said, and later, back home in bed when the room was dark, he said, "and I love the Lord." But he would not say directly, so the Lord would listen, "Lord, I love you, I love you, Lord." He wanted to, but he couldn't. Because the Lord would hear for sure if he was spoken to, and he would know it wasn't true, not the way it ought to be. Because Kelvin knew that from the dirt between his toes to the light brown of his coarse hair, with trembling and bad dreams, in all his secret thoughts from Sunday to Sunday, God saw him for what he was.

By the time he turned eleven he had thought more about it, and thought he would not be a preacher after all. He had thought about himself, how he kept doing things you go to hell for, and he knew that he wet the bed at night in punishment for that because there was no other reason. His grandfather knew about the bed, what everybody called the accidents, but he didn't know that they were acts of God.

Anyway Sunday got to be different for Kelvin, different from other days, so he couldn't be a preacher now if he wanted to be. For his grandfather, all days were the same, all days were Sunday in his blue serge suit and the way he would say "God bless you" to anyone without being embarrassed. When his grandfather said "God bless you" to the man at the filling station, Kelvin was embarrassed and knew he couldn't be a preacher.

He wished all days would be Sunday for him, too, but he thought about Saturday, which was where he stayed most of the time, the moving picture show and the vacant lot and the railroad track and the place under the loading platform at the cotton compress, where it was cool and you could smell cottonseed oil and dirt and spider webs, where Walter Thomas smoked cigarettes.

The immense unpainted platform, the floor for Negroes clumping over Kelvin's head, was the roof for Kelvin and Walter and O. D. who talked about girls and Joe Bob who sometimes had to work on Saturdays. O. D. had seen a girl naked and saw where babies came out and told Walter and Joe Bob and Kelvin. Walter and Joe Bob believed it and Joe Bob said he knew it already but Kelvin didn't say anything. He listened and picked his nose while the Negroes kept clumping on the ceiling, rolling cotton bales around the wide spaces between the boards of the platform, and fine powdered dirt would fall on Kelvin's head.

It was after such a Saturday and such a Sunday that Kelvin ate his oatmeal and got his books together and went to school on a bright November Monday morning. A wind was twisting the red leaves loose from the oak trees along Pickett Street. Kelvin walked in the gutter and plowed his feet through the leaves; splayfooted, he piled the leaves up ahead of him until there were too many to keep together and they spilled over and around his feet. He jumped over the pile he had made and started another one. He could look back and see a row of leaf hills, three or four in a block for that many blocks, before he turned the corner to head down Forrest Avenue, the rutted dirt road that led to the Woodrow Wilson School and the fifth grade classroom with George Washington unfinished on the wall and Miss Thackleberry, high, thin, and suspicious behind her desk.

It was a brown desk, heavy and old, and the names of students Kelvin guessed were a hundred years dead were cut into the front of it. The veneer had been ripped away in crooked strips and there were deep holes drilled in the top and long cuts the kind you might make if you were walking by the desk fast with a pocket knife at noon and there wasn't anybody else in the room. This morning when Miss Thackleberry, so skinny her cheeks sank in, was writing a note to Walter Thomas's father to get Walter a whipping for playing hookey two times, her pencil tore through the paper where the wood was gone. The lead snapped.

The students looked at her, their faces silent. She looked up, moving her sharp nose like a weathervane from left to right and back again. She looked across the tops of the students' heads toward the back of the room. She never frowned. Her face stretched tight around her bones.

"Let me have another sheet of paper," she said. Her long finger pointed at Walter's tablet then fell to her desk and started tapping. Walter didn't move and when she said it again she pinched the words off with lips so thin they were almost not lips. If God had been a woman, Kelvin thought, he would be Miss Thackleberry. She wadded the torn sheet, working with both her hands, ten squeezing worms, and dropped it into the gray metal bucket beside her desk. She finished the second note as the bell rang for morning recess, folded it neatly and gave it to Walter. He put it carefully into the chest pocket of his overalls and hurried to catch Kelvin and O. D., who were running for the best climbing tree on the school ground. When the bell rang again, and they were coming down, hanging from the low limbs and dropping to the hard earth, Walter said he was going swimming.

"Now?" Kelvin said. "Your daddy's gonna kill you plain out. You already got that note."

"That don't make no difference," Walter said. "My daddy gets aholter me, it ain't gonna matter anyway. Whippin' can't get no harder than it's already set to be."

"It's cold to go swimming," O. D. told him.

"Well, for you, maybe," Walter said. "Not for me. Ain't never too cold for me," and he was gone, across the dirt road and over a fence into a field of soybeans and over a low rise, waving with both hands high in the air so that Kelvin and O. D. saw him go down behind the rise that way, his head and arms and then his hands and then nothing.

Kelvin turned and moved toward the schoolhouse, his eyes on the smoke coming out of the brick chimney, his hands stiff-armed into his pockets. The fingers of his right hand made a fist around eight cat-eye marbles. His left hand rolled from finger to finger the cold sureness of his favorite steelie. In a way he was glad Walter had gone, because Walter always shot well, and during the month since school had begun Kelvin had lost some of his best marbles to him.

In the pencil groove of his desk Kelvin lined up the eight marbles, except the steelie, then let them roll one by one down the slant of the desk and off the edge into the palm of his hand. Miss Thackleberry lifted her eyes from the papers on her desk and stared into all the faces at once. Kelvin froze, relaxed, looked back at her, decided that was the wrong thing to do, and looked away. She dropped her eyes and went on grading papers.

Kelvin lined up the marbles again, this time with the steelie in the middle, and rolled them slightly, slowly, back and forth in the scarred trench. Then Ward West coming back from the pencil sharpener bumped the desk on purpose. Kelvin knew he was in trouble and that there was no way out. He knew the marbles would roll from the desk and run all over the floor. With one arm along the right side of the desk and another along the bottom, he tried to stop them.

The steelie rolling down the left side sounded like Pearl Harbor. He knew it would hit the floor like a cannonball if he didn't stop it. And then he knew as he shifted his arms to block the path of the steelie that: one, all of the marbles were going to get loose; two, Miss Thackleberry was staring at him standing up behind her desk hating him because he was not Suzie Long on the front row or Big Butt Berkle who always got to erase the board; and three, all the other pupils except Ward West were looking at him, glad because they were not him. Ward West, as big as a man, in overalls made of blue-striped mattress ticking, was staring at a book on his desk hearing the marbles roll and hit the floor and roll again. A girl giggled. Two girls giggled. Kelvin stopped trying to do anything about the marbles and sat still and put his hands in his lap. Then he realized there was a marble in his right hand. He wanted to get rid of it so bad he almost dropped it. He decided he was going to kill Ward West. He would make Suzie Long take all her clothes off and go to church and he would push Ward West with his yellowed teeth and black hair cut under a bowl into a bottomless pit. He would make them both go to church naked. He would turn them into Catholics and make them go to confession naked. He would turn Suzie Long into a naked nun, with all her sweet skin uncovered.

Miss Thackleberry was standing beside his desk.

"Well?" she said. She had said Well? to Kelvin more times than there were marbles in the world. "Well?"

"Yes ma'am?"

"Well?"

"Yes ma'am?"

"Don't you yes ma'am me."

"No ma'am."

"You watch your tongue, young man!"

Now was the time to stop answering, but it didn't matter. She was lifting him by a fistful of hair to pull him, head bowed and pained, to the front of the room. Then she straightened to all of her height, her neck stretched like a turkey's when it stops and takes air in the middle of the barnyard. She let go of his hair and looked down at him. Her brown-spotted bony hand swung out over the class and pointed down at the floor.

"Pick them up," she said without moving her lipless mouth.

She waited for all of Kelvin's eleven years while he hunted for the marbles. O. D. found two for him and when he handed them to him made a grotesque and sympathetic face. Kelvin handed six cat-eye marbles to Miss Thackleberry.

"The steelie," she said, her open hand waiting in front of his face. It was funny to hear her say "steelie." Kelvin wondered what she was like when she was a girl. He unwrapped his other hand from the big ball bearing and put it on her desk.

She sat down and put all the marbles in a drawer. Then she scooted back her chair with an awful noise and curled her fingers around the bumps of her knees. She looked Kelvin in the eyes, looked down into the kneehole of her desk and looked back into Kelvin's eyes.

"Well?"

Kelvin turned away from the class toward the blackboard. His feet floated into one another and his arms were full of water.

"Well?"

He took a short breath and let it out and got down into the kneehole in front of Miss Thackleberry's shoes. It was even smaller than he remembered from before when he had thrown a spitball and hit George Washington in the left eye, where it stuck. He drew his legs up and hugged them, closed his eyes and laid his head on the knobs of his knees. When Miss Thackleberry scooted the chair back into place to close the walls of his cell the sound scraped his skull. He shivered. When he opened his eyes Miss Thackleberry's knees were almost touching his forehead. They were moving slowly left and right. He watched them as they swayed, then jiggled and bounced a little and parted and came together again. Kelvin wanted to tell her he could see her pants, her ugly pants long all the way to her knees and yellow. Suzie Long's pants were panties he was sure.

Then he closed his eyes again, tried not to breathe and told himself that he was going to win, that he would not ask Miss Thackleberry to let him out. He would stay until the bell rang. He would go to sleep. He rested his forehead back on his knees and wished he had gone swimming with Walter.

He couldn't go to sleep because the smell was worse with his eyes closed. He held his breath as long as he could. Finally he said what he knew he would have to say and what Ward West was waiting for him to say. "Miss Thackleberry," he said, "please let me out."

She scooted the chair back and he crawled from the dark cave of the whale's stinking belly and stood up, sniffling. She took him by the arms and squeezed until the blood stopped.

"You aren't going to play with your marbles anymore?"

"No ma'am."

"Very well," she said, looking at him out of the cat-eyes in her head, but she didn't let go of him, and then the bell rang.

...

"Plee-hees let me out-out! Plee-hees let me out-out!" Ward West jeered and pointed and bumped into Kelvin as he ran past him on his way home. He knocked Kelvin across the sidewalk and into Dr. Layton's yard the pupils were warned not to step on.

Kelvin decided that he would tell his grandfather what he found out about love, how on the day when his grandfather had said, "Smile at the boy, Kelvin, let him know you want to be his friend. Beat him with love, son," Kelvin went to school sure of the invincibility of his partnership with his grandfather and God. Now he would tell his grandfather how on that very day he had turned every five or ten minutes to smile at Ward West who sat always in the back of the room, and how after school Ward West had beat him up for making faces at him.

"What happened, Boy?" his grandfather asked him.

"Nothing," Kelvin said.

"I tell you one thing," O. D. said at school the next morning, "you sure got a lot of courage. I'm not gonna go making faces at Ward West."

"You sure are brave," Suzie Long said, then ran away.

"You're crazy, you know that?" Ward West said.

Kelvin decided that when he got home this time he would tell his grandfather he was not going to be a preacher.

He took a long way home to stay away from Ward West. He stopped to watch a man change a tire and played touch football awhile with some boys from the junior high school but he was too little and they told him to go on home. There was a fire in the garage behind old man Hanson's house. Both the fire trucks came but Walter's father, who was a fireman, wasn't on either one of them. Kelvin figured he was busy whipping Walter. Mr. Hanson's Model T that was on cinderblocks, burned up.

There was a revival meeting in a tent by the cotton gin. The preacher was louder even than Kelvin's grandfather and took quick breaths every six or seven words and said "uh" all the time, "And the Lord-uh said-uh, I am the way-uh . . ." Kelvin stopped his bicycle and listened, and watching and listening he believed what he heard and wished it was him in the pulpit under the tent calling God down.

It was almost dark. Kelvin hurried past the three-story stone house near the water tower, staying in the middle of the street, away from shadows, because Walter had told him that the woman who lived there was half colored and half white and O. D. had said it was so. Kelvin saw her in his mind, black on one side and white on the other, one eye blue, one dark. He wondered what she sounded like when she talked, like a colored woman or like a white woman, and where she got all her money.

In Dr. Layton's yard, where no one was supposed to go, Kelvin saw O. D. standing in the grass with five or six other kids and a whole lot of grownups.

"You know what happened?" O. D. said.

He shook his head. "I been on my paper route."

"Walter got drowned."

"He what?"

"He got drowned."

"He didn't neither."

"He did, too. He got drowned this afternoon. That's where he is, right in there in Dr. Layton's office and so is all his whole family. His mother went and let out a big scream a while ago you could hear all over town."

"But I was just talking to him," Kelvin said, "just today at school."

"He was such a good boy," some woman said, and Kelvin knew that if they said Walter was such a good boy then O. D. was telling the truth and Walter was drowned. He thought about Walter breathing water and wondered if he was afraid, if he thought at the last second that he never would see his mother again.

Kelvin was afraid of water. He was glad that Methodists get sprinkled and not immersed except out in the country where his grandfather went. He knew if he was a Baptist he would have to go to hell.

Walter's family didn't come out of Dr. Layton's house, and pretty soon Kelvin's father found him and took him home to supper. He didn't have to eat anything and he went to bed early. He was afraid he would dream about Walter drowned but he didn't.

At the funeral at the Presbyterian church everybody walked by the coffin and looked in. Kelvin stopped when he got to the coffin and stared at Walter's eyelids to see if they moved so he could tell everybody and they would wake Walter up. He wanted to touch him but he was afraid to.

The woman behind nudged him and he went on with his father and mother and grandfather back to the pew.

The preacher said that God wanted Walter in heaven.

The choir sang "Asleep In Jesus" and a man sang "Nothing Between My Soul and My Savior." There were thousands of flowers and at first it smelled sweet like Easter Morning. Then they smelled sweet like vomit and the church was hot. The choir sang "Asleep in Jesus" again. Walter's mother cried and Kelvin thought how God only took Walter away because he wanted him, and he thought of Ward West who took away the raccoon Kelvin had brought to school and who always took whatever else he wanted.

He looked toward the casket again. A man he didn't know was putting the lid down.

When they got home, Kelvin sat on the front steps until he got a chill, then he went to bed without his supper again.

He closed his eyes and saw Jesus coming toward him. The swaddling clothes hung like rags. He could smell the frankincense and myrrh. Jesus moved his thin lips but there wasn't any sound. Kelvin got out of bed and went downstairs and told his grandfather he was not ever going to be a preacher. He went back to bed and lay awake a long time and didn't play with himself. In the morning he felt quickly to see and he saw that he had not wet the bed.

The Wall

"Man, you just don't know," John Oscar Carpenter said, passing from the shadows of the gym into the hard sunlight, barely turning to aim the words at Kelvin, standing guard in the doorway. "You don't know what you're missing." And the truth of the matter was just that. Kelvin Fletcher *didn't* know what he was missing. Maybe, if he had, he could have put it out of his mind. If he could have visualized the girls in their underthings, petticoats anyway, if he could have made the picture in his mind, he could have forgotten it. With no skirts on, or maybe less, but not naked—not with nothing on, no matter what John Oscar said. That was too much. Already, thinking about the girls in their small white or pink things, or whatever, it was almost impossible to sleep at night.

But mostly that was because John Oscar was right. Because he couldn't see them. Couldn't make them take shape. He tried to make them walk around the way they must walk on the other side of the wall, not knowing they are being looked at, easy and not embarrassed or conscious of themselves, but they wouldn't stay in place. It was like trying to imagine a dog running, really leg by leg imagine him running. It never looked right. He would try to focus on a girl and she slipped out of shape and spread out and twisted around until she didn't look like a girl anymore or anything at all, with a watermelon bottom and five or six breasts that kept crawling around her chest and belly like turtles.

Kelvin remembered how he used to take the little people shaped out of Kleen Klay at vacation Bible school and squeeze them together into a glob with only colors running through it and signs of heads and legs. That was the way the undressed girls in his mind kept contorting into one another.

John Oscar was right. If he had seen once for himself, if he could call to his mind the shape of one girl—of Salina Mae Becker—standing in front of him—Salina Mae Becker—he could say the way he heard Burnett Holloman, who didn't seem to believe it, say, "When you've seen one, you've see 'em all." But he couldn't say that. It wouldn't mean anything, because he hadn't seen one. He couldn't even imagine clearly what the boys looking through the hole in the wall were seeing. The trouble with him, and he knew it, was simply that he didn't know what he was missing.

Clement Long, for instance, who probably could see a girl in his mind like anything, never seemed interested in the wall that was this minute not quite stopping the sound of the girls on the other side. That might have been because Clement was too dignified. Not too dignified to look, of course, but to go climbing up the pile of tables and chairs and boxes that made the crooked tower leaning at a precarious angle against the partition. The wall divided the old gym into two oversize dressing rooms, and in the four months it had been put up most of the boys Kelvin knew had climbed at least once to the top of the tower to brace against the sheetrock almost twenty feet off the floor and look through the hole John Oscar had first thought of making.

During the last period of the day, girls from study hall came to the gym to shoot a few goals or tumble, and for a couple of hours after school the girls' basketball team and track team and the tumblers were prancing and jostling in and out of the gym, getting ready for the girls' track meet coming up in a few weeks, or simply making use of the field and equipment the boys monopolized during school hours at their own gym periods. After school the only boys were football players, and the track and mats and the main basketball court belonged to the girls. Some of them, at any one time—as John Oscar had noticed—were in the dressing room, changing their clothes.

The hole was so small that Kelvin could not see it from where he stood now at the door of the gym, watching for the approach of Coach Eberly. But he knew it was big enough and he knew that through it were seen wonders like nothing he had seen for a nickel at the Penny Arcade where the woman in black veils danced and didn't do anything else and only danced again for another nickel.

Once he had turned the crank a little at a time to see if she would move slowly and he could get used to her but she only changed from one frozen position to another as the picture cards flipped over. Both the nickels were for church, but he didn't do that often, almost never. There was nothing in it anyway because she was as old as his Sunday school teacher at least and because he was still saved then and was always afraid when he sinned. Afraid because he knew that his father even if he wasn't a preacher was an agent of God's secret service, that he was guided to evil as if he could see across town and through walls.

The only time Kelvin had slipped away from prayer meeting to spend his offering money on a movie he had felt his father's hand fall on his shoulder and it was as if a zombie had left the screen and slipped into the row of seats behind him. The only time he had smoked, when he was eleven, in the treehouse next door, his father had seen him from an upstairs window, and the sudden explosion of his voice calling Kelvin's name was too much like thunder from high above for Kelvin ever to forget the fear of God and His people.

Kelvin was not saved now, but he no longer fell much into sin. He walked into it. Twice he had gone to the show on Sunday. Yesterday he had told a dirty joke and listened to a better one. The thing was, you couldn't find out a lot of things without sinning and couldn't be much with anybody but God, and finally that wasn't enough anymore. He wasn't saved, but he knew what sin was and he still believed in it, and the thing was, he knew when he was sinning and didn't try to make it all right by explaining why it wasn't a sin the way Burnett Holloman always did.

He wondered sometimes if God like his father forgives you if you don't lie about what you did and admit it. He decided mostly when he thought about it that you still go to hell.

It was not God who had changed.

"Hey Kelvin!" Russell Goode said, stopping at the gym door and shifting a load of books in the crook of his arm. "C'mon, let's get a Coke."

"I can't," Kelvin said. "I'm watching."

"Did you get a turn?"

"No," Kelvin said, in the same matter-of-fact voice. "Seen one you've seen 'em all."

"And that's a crock, too," Russell said, shifting his books again. "You ain't seen 'em all till you've seen 'em all."

Kelvin meant to smile but it didn't straighten out right.

"Go on, grab a look," Russell said, moving into the shadow of the doorway. "I'll watch out for you."

"No, I can't. I told John Oscar I wouldn't go anywhere till he came back by."

"You're scared."

Kelvin shrugged and Russell Goode hefted his books again.

"I'm not exactly scared," Kelvin mumbled, almost too low to be heard.

"Then get on in there. Ain't nothing to worry about."

Kelvin looked at the tower and the boy on his knees high above them, looking into another world. He could feel his face flush and he was aware of his heart beating.

"Sure there's something to worry about," he said, turning his eyes back to brightness outside.

A red book dropped from under Russell's arm and Kelvin watched him pick it up as he talked. "Pay attention, Kelvin. Ain't a thing in the world can happen as long as somebody stays on the door."

"That's what *you* say."

"Well, what then?"

"I don't know," Kelvin said. "But sure as peedunk I'd get caught."

Ten minutes later John Oscar showed up.

"It's about time you got here," Kelvin said, jumping up from the squat he had dropped to when Russell left. His legs hurt when he straightened them and his right foot was asleep. "Goshdarn! I'll never make it in time."

"What's the matter? It's not even four."

"I got to get my homework before supper. It's Wednesday night."

"What's Wednesday night?" John Oscar asked, his face cranked around so he was looking out of the corners of his eyes.

"It's prayer meeting, stupid. Don't you know anything?"

"You have to go to *that*?"

Kelvin was supporting himself on his left leg, leaning against the building and holding his right foot suspended so it could come to as painlessly as possible.

"It's not so bad. Anyway, I don't guess it's going to hurt me," and he let his foot down and hobbled off, following the shadow of the school building, walking more naturally after the first few yards, then kicking stones aside, watching them roll and bounce out of his path. When he turned suddenly around the corner of the building, out of John Oscar's sight, he broke into a hard run.

...

His father was reading the newspaper and didn't look up. "You're late. School's been out an hour."

It hadn't been out that long, but Kelvin knew not to argue the point. He had fashioned his lie before he had run three blocks, and it came out easily. "Miss Verckle kept us to work on something. If we wanted to. You get extra credit."

"On what?" Paul Fletcher turned a page of the paper and folded it around with a snap of his long, heavy arms. He creased it and laid it in his lap and then he turned and looked at Kelvin leaning back against the front door, breathing heavily, his face redder than usual. Kelvin's right arm was bent behind him where his hand still clung tightly to the brass knob. "What were you working on?"

"For an assembly program. For Government."

"That going to help your grade?"

"It's extra credit."

"Well, you're going to *need* extra credit if you don't get your homework. Did you forget this is Wednesday night?"

"No sir, I remembered. I ran all the way home."

"I see you did. Where are your books?"

"I don't have to use them. All I have to do is practice a talk. And make up some problems for math. I don't need my books." It was a lie.

Kelvin was astonished and proud and ashamed that it had come so readily, with no sign of his own disgust that he had forgotten his books, left them at the gym door.

He would not be able to do his homework now, but it would be better to face his teachers than to anger his father.

"Well, you better get on it," his father said, and turned back to his paper. Kelvin went upstairs to his room and made up math problems until he was called to supper.

At prayer meeting he saw Salina Mae Becker and her mother. During a stand-up hymn he made a tube with his fist and looked through it at Salina Mae. He tried to imagine she was changing clothes but it didn't work. Then Brother Simmons prayed and talked about what prayer is for. Kelvin listened to him and forgot the hole in the wall and the girls. Before it was time for everybody to make a silent prayer Kelvin closed his ears to Brother Simmons and shut his eyes and prayed. He had moved his lips silently for no more than a few words when he knew God wasn't hearing him.

Later, in bed, he prayed again, and he felt better. He took his Bible from his lamp table and read something about principalities and became sleepy.

He woke up the next morning with the Bible under his face. He was sore where it had pressed against his cheekbone and left an impression on his freckled skin.

...

It was Thursday, and there was no need to rush home. There was still the Government assembly program to prepare for and there was no prayer meeting. He took the second watch at the gym door. The schoolyard, as much as he could see of it, was deserted, except for now and then a boy cutting across to the drugstore or coming over to wait for a turn at the tower. Kelvin kept his eyes open for any adults or any younger students who couldn't be trusted with a secret, and his ears were full always of the sounds of the four-man basketball game that went on whenever there was anyone on the tower. It was an excuse for the boys' presence in the gym after school every day, and they hoped too that it would make less noticeable the unavoidable sounds of tower-climbing that might carry over into the girls' side.

When he was relieved, a little after four, he didn't go home. He stepped inside the gym and watched the ball game for a few minutes and then he joined it and played until he heard a high laugh from the other side of the wall and gave up the ball and quit pretending. There were only two boys waiting at the tower and he got in line behind them. They were only allowed two minutes apiece if anyone was waiting, and Kelvin hoped someone would come behind him so that he would be forced to come down right away. Visions were swimming in his head, visions of himself freezing at the top of the tower, visions of being struck blind for looking. He knew that one quick look would be enough. He wanted to go up and to come down, with as little time between as possible.

The climb was not as easy as he had thought it would be. Nothing but gravity held the pieces of the tower together and he wasn't sure gravity was going to be enough. Jaybo West and Earl Dean Johnson helped him up and Harvey Lee Simpson the preacher's son steadied the furniture as well as he could, counter-balancing Kelvin's weight with his own until his hands wouldn't reach anymore. Twice Kelvin thought he was falling.

"Look out, stupid!" Earl Dean shouted in a whisper. "You're going to knock it over!"

Kelvin didn't breathe until the tower swayed slowly back into place. Behind the school he could hear the band practicing for Saturday's football game. He knew that in a little while they would be marching around the building and past the gym door. He started to climb down but he knew the boys would not forgive him for that, once he had started up.

It was not difficult to balance, after you got to the top. Kneeling on the plank that lay over the large box on the table supported by chairs that stood each on a box on a chair, he could lean forward comfortably with his hands and head braced against the wall and with his right eye precisely over the hole. The hole was so large now that he was afraid at first one of the girls would surely see it. But they never had and they wouldn't.

It took a second for the sight to register, then when it did he thought his heart would throw him down to the floor. *Oh God Jesus don't let anyone else get in line.*

The first thing was that some of the girls were sure enough naked. Three. Annette Freeman and Betty Sue House and a girl whose name he could never remember. The second thing was that almost everybody was standing and walking and laughing and talking the way boys do and he wondered if someone was going to pop someone's bottom with a towel. The third thing was Miss King the gym teacher in white shorts and white tennis shoes and taking her shirt off. The fourth thing was that Salina Mae Becker was not there. The fifth thing was that he had a hard-on and he had to squeeze his legs together or something but he knew that if he did he might fall. He heard the band marching past on its first circle around the building, stepping to fast drums.

Betty Sue House took a towel from a wooden bench and threw it over her shoulder and walked toward the shower stalls out of Kelvin's line of vision to his left. He noticed that her breasts were smaller than he had thought they would be. When she had disappeared he turned his eye back to Annette Freeman and saw with a strange delight that her breasts were larger than they had ever seemed and his single eye followed their rhythm as she followed Betty Sue's path toward the showers. Most of the girls were still in their white shorts and shirts, some already had showered and had their slips or dresses on or were getting into and out of things. Kelvin looked with slow long looks at long legs and navels and bright red nipples on soft tits that didn't crawl like turtles. He knew that if he didn't get down he was going to burst. He heard the band coming around the building again, all horns now, playing something loud and full of spirit.

Suddenly he felt dizzy. The tower seemed to sway to the right and then to the left and he looked down and saw that it was not him but the tower itself. Jaybo and Harvey Lee were doing their desperate best to right it and Earl Dean was holding his hands up as if he could calm it down the way a teacher shuts up a classroom full of children. Kelvin leaned gently against the wall and tried to brace himself and the tower together. The wood made a scraping noise against the sheetrock and Kelvin pushed the top of the tower out an inch from the wall. The band came closer, so close that Kelvin thought it was going to march straight in through the gym door and up to the wall but they turned and filed smartly past, trumpets playing alone, playing a wild music no man ever wrote.

Then the wall gave way. Slowly at first, leaning over toward the girls, bulging with Kelvin's weight. Then to each side of him the wall cracked, leaving a large center section leaning far out over the dressed and half-dressed and undressed girls, running back from it, standing aghast, covering themselves with hands and towels. Kelvin looked back in terror to see the rear ends of three blue jeans, one white shirt tail flying, fade into the sunlight. The corner of his eye caught the abandoned basketball still rolling across the floor. The tower held now, leaning and falling with the broken section, and kept him from sliding down the slanting wall and running on broken ankles after his friends.

Then the wall fell and Kelvin rode it down. There was a whoosh of air rushing from beneath it. He heard a girl scream and in the distance he heard marching music.

The last thing he saw of the world zooming toward him was a long bare arm with a finger pointing at a boy falling out of the sky. Then he hit and there were explosions in his knees. The first thing he saw when the nausea passed was someone not himself on all fours in the middle of the girls' dressing room, his face still centered over the gigantic hole in the sheetrock as Miss King, in white shorts and white tennis shoes and socks and nothing else at all beat him viciously over the head with a towel. The teacher was making sounds Kelvin couldn't understand and in her eyes there was a look of more than rage. She held the towel like a club in both hands and swung it again and again at the motionless unbelievable head. Two shapes hid behind her and vaguely to his right what was left of Rosemary Rutledge crouched down, her chin between her knees, eyes and mouth wide open and locked, her panties clutched forgotten in her white fist.

The room turned over and there was no one left but the teacher and the boy and Rosemary. Miss King swept the room with her eyes and screamed at the girl. "Get out of here, you little idiot! Get out of here and get your clothes on!"

Then there was no one left but the teacher and the boy, and gradually Kelvin Fletcher knew who the boy was.

The principal had gone home but Miss King telephoned him. As Kelvin waited with her in the office where still she spoke not a single word to him, he thought of the two things that took over his mind. That now Salina Mae Becker would never want him, and that it didn't matter anyway because his father was maybe going to kill him, and if his father didn't he would do it himself.

"I told you!" he screamed in his mind at Russell Goode and all the legs disappearing into the sun. "I told you I always get caught!"

Already he could feel the powerful grip of his father's hand on his shoulders. He looked at the rough grain of the desk and the patterns in the tile floor and knew that his father would not kill him and that he would not kill himself either, and the thing now, since he would have to live through it and since there was no choice but to tell the truth, was how much his father would understand about sin.

There Aren't Any Foxes in That Cave

His mother's dead, his face is red,

Kelvin Fletcher wets the bed . . .

None of it was true. Kelvin Fletcher's mother was alive. And there had been no accidents for nearly four years. He used to believe his problem was a secret, but gradually he came to painful awareness that just about everybody knew. The way they knew Walter Thomas had a crazy uncle and that Mr. McPherson drank whiskey and Josephine Owens had to get married. Kelvin remembered the sheets with their round stains hanging above the chickens in the back yard, getting dry in the sun, telling his secret in ugly waves to the people passing down the side street. He remembered wishing that his public shame was a crazy uncle or that he drank whiskey or had to get married. Then at least he could have camped out, or spent the night with friends. Now it was four years past, but sometimes it was suddenly with him again, like a whiff of those yellowed sheets.

Kelvin squatted beneath the window and looked through the stiff white curtains at the lot across the street. It sounded like the choir from church, chanting the rhyme over and over. But it was only John Oscar Carpenter whom he hated already and Jaybo West whose father cut wood for beer money and Burnett Holloman who was a doctor's son.

Then Harvey Lee, whose father was Brother Simpson the preacher, stopped on his bicycle and talked to the three for a minute. Kelvin imagined that he was telling them what it meant to be a Christian, but he must have said something else because they all laughed and got on their bicycles and everybody was gone.

Kelvin went back to his bedroom and started packing again. The suitcase was his father's and too big, but that was better than using his mother's, which was blue. Anyway he wouldn't see the thing after he got to Mount Carmel. He wouldn't see anything but the mountain and the trees and the sunset at Inspiration Point. It was the first church camp he'd ever been to, because he didn't stop wetting the bed until he was thirteen. But now the kids across the street chanting that rhyme had been lying. And he was going to Mount Carmel.

"Here!" he said when his name was called, more quickly than he meant to. And Clement Long, who never came to church except for hay rides and Easter, said "Here!" when his name was called, climbed into the bus, and sat down beside Kelvin. "These seats'll cook your ass off!" Clement said. Kelvin kept looking out the window because he didn't know how to talk to Clement, who was seventeen and in the eleventh grade and had been kicked out of school once.

"This is the first time you been?"

Kelvin turned at the question and looked at Clement, who seemed even older than seventeen, and wore a tie, and who would smile like you were his best friend. He knew that Clement, who used bad language and hardly ever came to church, was against Jesus.

You're not even a Christian, he wanted to say. What are you coming here for? Because the more he thought about it, the more he resented Clement, who would come every year, while Kelvin, whose right it was, had had to wait so long. But he said, "I haven't been to this camp, but I went to lots in Booneville, where I come from."

"What you gonna do up there?"

It was a stupid question, and Kelvin didn't know how to answer it. He looked out the window again and shrugged his shoulders and watched the cotton rows running by like caterpillar legs.

"I don't know. What you gonna do?"

"I'm gonna do right," Clement said, "and talk to Jesus." And he settled back into his seat. The bus turned north and the morning sun hit Kelvin in the face. He settled back too, and looked sideways at Clement: his eyes were closed, and his mouth was set in the kind of grin Kelvin made when he pretended to be The Shadow. He closed his eyes and said, making the words silently with his lips, "Help this person." He felt the light from the sun, cut on and off by a row of oaks, flash across his eyelids. Then it sank deep into his skin until he was sleepy. He thought of his own promises to do right. He thought of how many times, especially this year, temptation had come over him and he had to pray for help and close his eyes against the world. It had seemed at times that something inside him was not saved at all, something that sneaked around in his head like the boys he had seen writing ugly words on sidewalks. In school when always the same girl went to the board and pointed to the right answer he sinned in his heart. This partly was why he had come to Mount Carmel. God's mountain, Brother Jenkins called it. Thinking, he felt the guilt again and then the broken light of the sun like the fingers of God washing him clean. Kelvin knew he had done the right thing, coming to the mountain.

"Hey . . . hey!" Clement was shaking him. "We're here!"

Kelvin thought for a moment that he had wet his pants, then he realized it was only where he had sweated. He sat up to look out the window for the first sight of the mountain. Reflected in the glass window of a bus from one of the other churches, parked only a couple of feet away, Kelvin gawked back at himself. He started to get up and then he thought how strange it was to see himself sitting in the other bus and he looked again. There he was, clear and solid. He thought, what if he was the reflection and the Kelvin Fletcher on the other bus was the one thinking all this. Then he remembered Clement and looked over the other Kelvin Fletcher's shoulder at the boy who was leaning over to see whatever it was out there. Kelvin looked at the two faces together, Clement's black in the depth of the glass and his own pale, almost white. Then into his face suddenly came the face of a girl. Her long brown hair hung from the head of Kelvin's reflection and framed his face. Together they looked like a picture of Jesus fastened to the side of the bus. Then the face of Jesus smiled, or was it the girl?

"What are you doing?" Clement said. "Let's get out of here. It's hot as hell."

By the time Kelvin had taken his bags from the bus and adjusted his eyes to the light and counted his money, all the other boys except Clement had paired off into cabinmates. He was sorry for Clement, who was not popular with the boys because he played too rough for somebody as big as he was and made fun of you and didn't seem to want to be friends. But Kelvin didn't feel sorry for himself; he knew why no one had chosen him. It meant something to him to be a Christian, and the other kids felt uncomfortable when they used bad words or told dirty stories around him. And that was how, as Kelvin would recall it, he and Clement Long got to be cabinmates. Kelvin, for his part, was not displeased. The more he thought about it, the more he saw another power at work.

...

The cabin they were assigned to was down a dirt walk about fifty yards from the director's white frame home, which was also the administration building. The cabin seemed to sit lopsided on the large natural stones that supported its corners, and the paint was curling up into hundreds of green flakes stuck to the rough wood of its walls. The room smelled like pine and cedar, but there was a mustiness about it, like an old trunk. The only ventilation was a single four-paned window over one of the army-cot beds. The window was hinged at the top and was propped open now with a broken broomstick. It reminded Kelvin of the door of a rabbit trap he and his father had made once. There were rusted nails in the walls, two pine trees he could touch if he reached out the window, a bare bulb hanging from the ceiling by an old cloth-wound electric cord, and an army blanket folded neatly at the foot of each naked mattress.

"What a whorehouse!" Clement said, as he dropped his suitcase on the bed by the window and lay down beside it.

Kelvin was embarrassed and didn't understand so he didn't say anything.

"But you know," Clement informed him, "this old mountain can be a great place when you find your way around."

Kelvin was unpacking, hanging his clothes in the dusty wardrobe. He decided he would have to say something, so he said in a low voice aimed at the coat hanger in his hand, "I guess it is. Russell Goode says there's a cave down under Inspiration Point a ways where a fox lives."

"A what?"

"A fox."

"There aren't any foxes around here."

"Well, I don't know, but he said he saw one."

"Wake up, Kelvin. Russell Goode says anything. Who did he take to the cave?"

Kelvin closed his father's suitcase and put it under his bed and loaded his hands with toothpaste and soap and things and went into the small bathroom. He had not expected to hear this kind of language at a church camp, even from Clement, and he wondered if he ought to wait, if this was the time to call Clement down, to tell him what kind of life he was headed for. But he didn't understand what Clement meant by "Who did he take?" He decided it would be all right to say so, and did.

"I mean what was her name?" Clement said.

"Whose name?"

"Kelvin, you're kidding me. Nobody's that dumb."

Kelvin was standing in the door of the bathroom confused and offended. He pushed his hands deep into his pockets and then he shrugged as if he didn't care what Clement thought anyway and took a few jellybeans out of his pocket. He tossed one onto Clement's bed and rolled the rest of them in his fingers like marbles.

"Come on, Kelvin. I mean the tail . . . the girls." Clement sat up on the side of the bed and a new look came over his face. "You haven't ever had any tail, have you?"

"So what if I haven't?"

"So never mind. You don't know what I'm talking about."

Kelvin drew back and straightened a little and carefully formed the right question, the perfect challenge that would make Clement's walls come tumbling down. He said, "What did you come here for?" the way a lawyer would say it.

"You want me to tell you?"

"I asked you."

Clement looked as if he were thinking of something pleasant and far away and fell back on his pillow and locked his hands behind his head. "To walk with Jesus," he said.

"You take the Lord's name in vain," Kelvin said. It was an announcement and an accusation and a warning all together. Kelvin had raised his voice, and now he was trembling. He hoped Clement wouldn't realize it, and he tossed a jellybean into the air and Clement caught it.

"You know what you need, Kelvin? You need about twenty minutes in the bushes."

"What you need," Kelvin cut in, "is to know what it means to be a Christian and that's something you sure don't know."

"OK," Clement said, resigned. He kicked off his loafers and stuck the jellybean into his mouth.

"Proverbs twenty-eight, eighteen."

"What's that supposed to mean?"

Kelvin took his Bible from beside his pillow and opened it to Proverbs and laid it on Clement's belly. Slowly, as if he were doing Kelvin a small favor that he found boring, Clement found the passage and read:

> *Whosoever walketh uprightly shall be saved, but he that is perverse in his way shall fall at once.*

   ...

     That morning they registered, then for a lunch of beans and wieners in the screened-in dining hall they stood in a long and restless line along the only concrete walk on the mountain. Later there were classes on Christian Discipleship and Program Planning and Recreation. When Kelvin got back to his cabin a little before suppertime, Clement was lying on the bed reading a paperback book. He raised one finger in greeting without taking his eyes from the page and Kelvin touched his hand to his eyebrow the way generals salute each other. He sat down on the side of his bed and began to read his Bible.

  "You're not supposed to move your lips," Clement said a few minutes later.

  "I'm not moving my lips."

  "Yes you are. Look, I'll show you. Read this paragraph right here. Read it to yourself."

  Suspiciously, trying to appear sure of himself, Kelvin reached for the book. He was not going to be corrected by this boy who was a sinner. He would be the teacher. This room would be his own parish and he would crush out evil. Clement leaned over and pointed to the paragraph:

> Her mouth was hot against mine. She writhed like a saint on fire,
> her fingernails tore into my flesh. With quick, easy motions I
> unzipped her dress and slipped it off . . .

  Kelvin took a slow breath and with great long-suffering patience handed the book back to Clement and went into the bathroom and washed his hands for supper.

"You moved your lips again," Clement said.

Kelvin went back to his bed and unfolded a mimeographed lesson plan from the afternoon's class and looked at it without reading.

He wanted to go home. He spoke defensively, and he didn't like the sound of his voice. "You don't know everything," he said, and he meant to let it go at that, but he couldn't. "I know what's wrong with you."

"How did you get to be a brain doctor?"

"You're going to hell, Clement Long. You know that?"

Clement locked his fingers over his belly and looked up at the ceiling. "I can't say I do. I don't know much about hell. But I'll tell you what, Kelvin. I'm gonna give you a chance to be born again . . . brother." He swung a pointed finger slowly around until it was aimed at Kelvin's face. "I'm gonna get you a girl tonight."

"I don't want a girl," Kelvin mumbled.

"Well what *do* you want."

Kelvin stood up, put his hands in his pockets, and walked across the floor. He took a deep breath and let it out slowly so that his voice would be even, untroubled and convincing.

"I want what I came here for. You're going to laugh, but I want to know Jesus Christ. And that's all."

"You don't want to know Salina Mae Becker?"

Kelvin stood facing his tormentor. "Tell me something," he said, and there was doom in his voice. He looked down from his pulpit, the echo of his words booming from the rafters, and out of his pocket a finger came that pointed directly at Clement. "Do you believe in God?"

"I don't know."

"Then why did you come here?"

"You're really serious."

"You can't answer that, can you?"

"You bet I can answer it. There's more tail on this mountain the first two weeks in August than anywhere else in the state."

Kelvin's face was glowing. "I feel sorry for you, Clement," he said. His words were stretched thin with anger.

Clement went into the bathroom and turned the water on in the sink and started to unbutton his shirt. "I'm going to tell you something you won't believe, Kelvin. I appreciate what you said, that you feel sorry for me, because I know you mean it."

Kelvin was uncomfortable now. "Just never mind," he said. "Just drop it."

"I mean, you've still got hold of mama's tit. That's all. Nothing wrong with tits, but you ought to let go of mama's and get someone your own age." Clement lathered his face and started to shave.

"I think maybe it's you never got off the bosom," Kelvin said, and realized he was relaxing. He had told Clement the truth, had put him in his place. He spoke in his own voice. "Why don't you forget about—bosoms—and hold on to The Cross? Did you ever think of that? I guess you think it's corny."

"No, I don't think it's corny. Only you don't get splinters from Salina Mae Becker."

"I don't get anything from Salina Mae Becker." It was as good an answer as Clement's.

"I'll bet you could, though," Clement said. "I'm taking her roommate out tonight. Why don't you get Salina Mae and come with us?"

Kelvin felt a glass of cold water spill in his stomach. He ate a jellybean. Clement finished shaving and sat shirtless, buffing a pair of shoes.

"Well?"

"Salina Mae is a nice girl."

"Sure she's a nice girl. And talk about bosom. Man, there's a cross I could bear. Matter of fact . . ."

"I got to study," Kelvin said. He picked up his Bible.

"You gonna study that?"

"So what?" He was disappointed in himself, but mostly he was disturbed because God had not put words into his head as his mother had told him would happen.

"Well look. We'll take it with us. I'll even carry it for you. You carry these." Clement took from his wallet four bright silver disks that looked like toy money and held them out. Kelvin put his hands into his pockets again and turned the last jellybean in his fingers. Clement shrugged. "ok," he said, "forget it. She probably wouldn't have let you anyway."

"I hope she wouldn't," Kelvin said, and in his mind he was bearing her, naked, arms spread like a cross, slowly up Mount Carmel. He lay down on the bed and closed his eyes and hoped that now the conversation would come to an end. Clement went to the bathroom and got into the shower.

Moving suddenly, as if he had heard a signal, Kelvin picked up the pants Clement had tossed onto the bed, found the silvered disks, and put them into his own wallet. Then he sat down again with the Bible and looked at the pages, at the swirling patterns where Revelations ought to have been. He kept looking as Clement, getting dressed, said, "You're reading in bad light," and left.

He thought a long time of what he had done, that he had kept a girl from being hurt. He wondered why he didn't feel good. Maybe, like Jesus, he had taken her shame upon himself.

It was then he thought about Clement's book. If this was where Clement's thoughts were coming from, it had to be destroyed because he wanted to help Clement. When they were talking, just for a minute, Kelvin had felt he was talking to his own brother. But he didn't have a brother. And if he did it wouldn't be Clement. Clement had flat eyes. Kelvin's brother would have his mother's eyes, with the fires of righteousness blazing in them, and love. Kelvin had these eyes. So, they said, did Dwight Moody and Billy Sunday. It was a gift, and it was an obligation.

The book was lying face down, where Clement had put it, open to the same page. Kelvin sat cross-legged on his bed, leaned back against the wall, and began to read. He would have to be sure of what he was doing. To God and to himself and maybe to Clement, he would have to justify destroying the book. He would study it now, when he was calm and there was no one around.

With quick, easy motions I unzipped her dress and slipped it off
her shoulders. It fell to the floor. Without taking her eyes off mine,

she stepped out of it and took off her brassiere and tossed it at my face, and her high, pointed breasts jerked once and settled. I could almost feel the nipples pressed in the palms of my hands. She opened her mouth, barely, and put her tongue between her lips and slipped out of her panties. Then, tall creature of the earth, mother of men, she offered them to me as she backed slowly, very slowly, toward the . . .

In the bathroom, with the door to the cabin locked, Kelvin masturbated. Afterward he tore the pages from the book and flushed them down the toilet, and walked into the woods and hid the cover of the novel under a stone.

He had promised God, and here on God's mountain he had sinned again. And now the shame was worse because he was certain that Clement, even Clement, did not do this. He wondered what rhymes they would say for him if they knew; if his father was right and it made you crazy. But at least the guilt was his and the girl had not been hurt.

He looked in the mirror, and he was frightened. My God my God why hast thou forsaken me? The fires of righteousness had gone out. Maybe he was only tired. Maybe there had never been any fires at all. He lay down on his bed and cried.

. . .

Standing in line for supper, Kelvin pulled his meal ticket from his wallet, and three of the silvered disks fell out. Two landed at his feet. He stepped on them both, spreading his legs between them until he looked like a new colt trying to stand, or a child with his pants wet. He stood like this, waiting for the end of the world, as the third silvered disk rolled down the walk, past Brother Jenkins and Mrs. Jenkins, past John Oscar Carpenter and Brother Simpson and Rosemary Rutledge, who picked it up and dropped it. Kelvin thought of scooting the disks under his feet all the way to the dining room and on to the table where he would eat. But when he slid his foot the impossible thing beneath it stayed where it was. He thought he could make his heart stop, but he couldn't. He wanted to know if everyone was looking at him, but he couldn't lift his eyes. Then the line moved, and he had to move with it. The three disks lay there on the walk, glistening.

At his table, where he ate nothing, Earl Dean Johnson passed by with his tray and said, "Old Fletcher done gone and fooled *everybody* . . . hey, boy?" John Oscar sat down at the table and said, "You sneaky little bastard," and put one of the rubbers under the salt shaker and passed it to Kelvin. Patsy Morgan whispered to Annette Freeman and they made prune-lipped grins. Then Kelvin got a note to see Brother Jenkins immediately after the meal.

Brother Jenkins nodded to a wicker chair and Kelvin sat down in it. It gave a couple of inches and squeaked as if it were alive.

"Kelvin," Brother Jenkins began, "I don't quite know what to say to you." He dropped into a large oak swivel chair that squeaked on its spring louder than Kelvin's chair but in a different voice. "I know what I *ought* to say, of course, but I can't believe I have to. I just don't understand how this could have happened. We've all thought of you as a fine young man. Every one of us would have said there's not a finer Christian boy on the mountain. Do you know that?"

It was not something Kelvin wanted to say yes or no to. He pulled his shoulders up almost imperceptibly as if he were about to shrug them and looked down at the pine floor.

"The fact is, you've been an example, I mean a real Christian soldier. I feel like one of our best men has been wounded in battle. That's really the way I feel, Kelvin, so you see I'm not angry with you. I want to help you heal your wounds. If you'll let me. Do you understand?"

"Yes, sir."

"Because there are a lot of battles ahead. God needs you."

Through the window Kelvin heard the smack of a bat against a softball and the screams of the girls cheering someone around the bases. He wished the ball would fly into the window and knock something over.

"You're thinking that I don't understand, Kelvin, but I *do* under-stand." The preacher shifted and the spring let out a short cry.

"Yes, sir."

"We know the thoughts that go through the minds of boys and girls your age. And our Lord knew, Kelvin. 'Lead us not into temptation but deliver us from evil.' He was speaking for all of us. What we have to remember, Kelvin, is that sex . . .

" . . . is not something dirty. It's something beautiful which God has given us to bring His children into the world. There is a part of us the devil always tries to get hold of to make us take these joys for ourselves. But they are not ours, you see. They are God's. We must be stewards. We have to wait for those pleasures God reserves for marriage. We have to wait, don't you see, not because sex is bad, be-cause it isn't and you must remember that. We have to wait because it's a beautiful and sacred thing, an instrument of God. Do you see that, Kelvin? Do you understand?"

"Yes, sir." But he was sure his mother would think it was bad. Maybe his father, who had never said anything, knew it was too sa-cred to talk about. He would have to think this over.

"We have to draw on the strength of our heavenly Father, Kelvin, because it isn't easy to do the right thing. The Lord said 'Not my will but thine be done.' You remember—he was on a mountain, too."

"Yes, sir."

Brother Jenkins leaned forward across the desk. The swivel cried again and the preacher lowered his voice almost to a whisper.

"Kelvin, have you made any use of those things, here on this mountain?"

"No, sir. I haven't ever used them anywhere."

"You're telling me the truth?"

"Yes. Yes, sir."

"Well, thank God for that." Then he looked sideways at Kelvin and sniffed and scratched his nose. "What were you doing with them?"

"I don't exactly know. I just sort of picked them up."

"You found them and you picked them up."

"Yes, sir."

"It was a novelty, maybe a little daring, to have them in your pocket. Is that it?"

"I guess so. Yes, sir."

"Well, that's perfectly normal, Kelvin. But it puts you in the way of temptation, don't you see?" He closed his eyes and pinched the bridge of his nose. When he spoke again his voice was more direct. "I'm just telling you to stay away from temptation. Because there's such a thing as sin, Kelvin. Sin is as real as you are. You make up your mind you're going to do what God wants you to do, to save yourself for some fine young woman who is saving herself for you at this very moment. Be the kind of example the other boys can follow. Will you do this?"

"Yes, sir."

Brother Jenkins locked his fingers under his chin and leaned forward. His eyes closed again. "We beseech Thy help for this young man. Keep his heart pure with the light of Thy love. In the name of Jesus. Amen." As Kelvin and the preacher stood up, the chairs cried out once again and were quiet. "Do you have any more of those things?"

"No, sir." And Kelvin knew it was the most important lie he had told.

On the way back to the cabin he saw Mrs. Jenkins, who smiled at him like she was being eaten by lions, and Poppy Selben, who didn't look at him at all. A boy he didn't know said, "Hey, Stud!" Burnett Holloman and Harvey Lee Simpson asked him what the old man said, and walked with him halfway to the cabin.

. . .

"You son of a bitch!" Clement closed the door to the cabin and leaned back against it, stiff and motionless, a stunned look on his face. "You stupid son of a bitch. You know what you did?"

It had been dark for a long time. Kelvin was lying in bed waiting. He seemed to be staring through the ceiling.

"I took those things."

"Kelvin, I know you took them! I had to go bareback. You know what that could mean?"

Kelvin thought of Clement lying between the long white legs, somewhere under the trees.

"It means you went ahead and did it."

"It means if that girl gets pregnant I'm going to knock your head off."

Clement kicked free of his loafers and sat down on his bed. He rested his chin on his fists and closed his eyes.

"Why, Kelvin? Why did you let me go out there with no rubbers? What were you trying to do?"

Kelvin wondered how the girl looked, and thought of Clement going through his wallet trying to find the things, and then falling on her. He wondered what you do first, and what you say when it's over.

"I don't know," he said. "I had a talk with Brother Jenkins . . ." he began to fool with the button on his pajamas.

"You told him?"

"No, I didn't mention you . . . there were all those people at supper."

"Kelvin, if you'll just tell me why you took them, and try to tell me what you're talking about, maybe I won't kill you."

Kelvin moved his hand up to another button, and then he turned his eyes to the bump his feet made under the blanket. He wiggled his toes, then stopped because he didn't want Clement to think he wasn't taking the conversation seriously.

He shrugged and drew his legs up and pulled his elbows into the curve of his belly and dropped his head down. He looked like an Indian about to be buried.

"Kelvin, did you hear what I said?"

"I wanted to see them."

"I don't believe you."

"I can't help it. It's the truth."

"Do you have a girl?"

"Not exactly."

"Look Kelvin. I'm going to tell you one more time. Because I like you—though God knows why—I won't kill you if you'll just let me in on what you're talking about."

Kelvin looked up to see what expression Clement had on his face but there wasn't any. Clement was busy scratching mosquito bites.

"What about the preacher?"

"The things fell out of my billfold in the lunch line. He was there."

"My God, Kelvin. Why don't you just take a gun and shoot yourself?"

"I might. I haven't decided."

"What did you tell him?"

"Nothing."

"Well, maybe you can live after all. But the thing is, I'd have been glad to loan you one. You didn't have to take them all."

"Well, anyway, I'm sorry."

"OK, OK. Forget it. But I'm just a little hacked off that you've got a girl and put on this big act and then don't let me in on it."

"That's not it."

"Well, what is it?"

"I don't know."

"Well, I do. I think the old boy came alive tonight and went out hunting himself a girl and was ready for three. I think the old boy got himself all hot and bothered and went looking for salvation. That's what I think. And you know what? I forgive you. Yes sir, Kelvin Fletcher—you are—forgiven! Did you get a piece?"

Kelvin looked at him, wide-eyed. Clement grinned.

"No, I guess you didn't." He scratched his chest like a monkey and yawned.

"Anyway, welcome."

"To what?"

"Why, to the human race, Kelvin, to the human race."

Clement unbuttoned his shirt and threw it on the foot of his bed. He pushed the front of his belt down and began scratching around a mosquito bite on the edge of his navel. Then he felt the itch on his back and then on the leg again. So he took off his pants and laid them on the bed, scratching with both hands. He let out a groan of pleasure and reached down into his socks with each hand and worked viciously on his ankles.

"I'll tell you one thing, Kelvin. There aren't any foxes in that cave."

"You sure found some mosquitoes, though."

"Just a couple," Clement said, "but they came on like a plague. I kept telling them I wasn't a Jew. I was a Christian. Christians don't get plagues, do they?"

"I don't think so. I think they just go to hell."

Later they lay in bed a long time without talking. And later, when the locusts seemed to scream in the trees, Clement got up and closed the window and took a cigarette from his suitcase and lit it.

"Tell me something, Kelvin. Did you suddenly decide you wanted a girl, or have you been a phony all this time?"

"I don't know," Kelvin said. "I don't know for sure what I want."

"Well I do."

"Do you think I've lost my religion, Clement?"

"Probably."

"But how do you tell? Because when I think about it, I'm still sentimental about Jesus."

"So am I, Kelvin. Who isn't?"

They didn't say anything else.

Clement put out his cigarette and Kelvin wrapped his cover tightly about himself and thought of his mother and of Salina Mae Becker. And then a sudden rain came down on the woods, and the locusts stopped their screaming.

Cantaloupes

After washing his tennis shoes, Kelvin Fletcher had tied the strings of the two together and hung them over a clothesline to dry. Even in the August sun it took more than four hours, and though he had made a bow knot, the shrinking of the laces made them difficult to separate. He was already running late. He didn't want to make Roy Dean Cummins wait on him.

Roy Dean had moved to town only a couple of months ago, and he was already popular in school.

"He seems awfully nice," mothers would say when they met him. And he did. He was as nice as anybody Kelvin Fletcher had ever met. But he was also very smart—he was ahead of the class he came into—and he was good-looking in a way that Kelvin had always wanted to be.

Still, the mothers were right to like him. He always said "Yes, ma'am" and "May I, please?" and smiled at them.

Sometimes, when he saw how the girls at school liked to be with Roy Dean, Kelvin didn't want to like him at all, but he did anyway. Everybody did. He was just a nice person.

This was Kelvin's first chance to get to know him better, maybe even to be friends with him, although Roy Dean didn't really seem to have any friends, strange as that was, considering that he was the center of things wherever he went—a dance after school, where he danced better than anybody else but never showed off, or just at the snack shop, where he fed the juke box but didn't usually choose the records.

When Jennie Thornburg invited the whole class for a picnic out at her place—a big farm the river bends around—Roy Dean asked how to get there. He didn't ask Kelvin, exactly. He asked whoever heard him, and Kelvin answered.

It would have been simple enough to draw a map, but Kelvin said he would ride his bicycle and that Roy Dean could ride along with him. He expected Roy Dean to say, "Why don't you just draw me a map?" but instead he said, "That'll be fine; thank you very much."

"I'll come by your house," Kelvin said. "What time? About nine?"

"You don't know where I live."

"No."

"I'll meet you in front of the school. No need for you to go out of your way."

"About nine?"

"How far is it?"

"Pretty far."

"Whenever," Roy Dean said. A little impatiently, Kelvin thought, but not unkindly.

And soon they would be together, riding side by side, talking about things. Everybody at the party would see them riding up together.

He got the laces separated and the shoes on his feet and was on the bicycle in time to get to the schoolyard by ten after nine, no matter that he hadn't taken time for breakfast.

Roy Dean was waiting for him, sitting on the grass, watching cars go by, his bicycle lying on its side behind him. He didn't seem irritated. He just smiled.

They rode the first mile in silence.

"Do you like it here ok?" Kelvin asked.

"Sure," said Roy Dean.

Then they rode in silence a while longer.

"Are you going to go to college?" Kelvin asked.

"Sure," said Roy Dean.

And so forth.

Then they rode in silence a while longer.

And then the chain on Roy Dean's bicycle broke. Kelvin offered to walk with him to push their bikes the rest of the way. Roy Dean wouldn't hear of it. Then Kelvin offered to carry Roy Dean on his bike the rest of the way, with the other one hidden in the woods.

"Let's hitchhike," Roy Dean said. "If we can hide one, we can hide them both. We can come back later and pick them up."

"We'll have to hide them real good," Kelvin said. "I had to save two years to buy mine."

"We'll cover them with leaves. Don't worry about it."

"I'm not worried."

The place was marked in their minds by telephone poles and a silo, and the bicycles were chained together to a small tree and buried under all manner of leaves and limbs.

Kelvin and Roy Dean stood for an hour with their thumbs out, with no luck at all. Once four girls in a blue convertible, girls not from their school, slowed down and threw them kisses and laughed and then speeded up and left them.

"Bitches," Roy Dean said. "Friggin' bitches."

"Bitches," Kelvin said.

Roy Dean looked sidewise at Kelvin and barely smiled.

"If I was in a car and they were walking," Kelvin said, "I would have picked them up."

"No kidding," Roy Dean said. He walked across the country road and set himself to hitchhike in the other direction.

"You're not going to the party?" Kelvin asked him, raising his voice to speak across the road.

"By the time we got a ride, there wouldn't be any party."

"I guess not."

"Come on," Roy Dean said. "I'll buy you a beer."

Kelvin had never had a beer.

A farmer stopped in a pickup truck that must have been as old as the man. A loose front fender bounced and clanged when the idling engine shook the frame of the truck. The farmer had a large brown dog in the front seat, so there was room for only one more. Roy Dean insisted on getting in the back, with a load of cantaloupes, and told Kelvin to get in the cab.

This was partly, Kelvin surmised, because the old man smelled bad. They could tell that as soon as they opened the door, even on the passenger side. It wasn't the dog. Kelvin saw Roy Dean wrinkle his nose.

They drove as slow as the man talked, dragging out his words and forgetting what he had said. He talked mostly about his family, the wife poorly, the son and daughter gone, and about the county, how much it had changed, about his dog, and then Kelvin stopped listening. He looked around and saw Roy Dean lobbing a cantaloupe into the woods that ran beside the road, then another one. Kelvin was terrified. When he gathered the nerve, a couple of miles later, to look again, the pale dirty orange balls were flying in easy arcs, one to the left, then to the right, then to the left. He saw then, with guilty relief, that the side view mirror had no glass in it and the rear view mirror hung swaying in its socket. When he looked again, cantaloupes were dropping over the side like bombs from Roy Dean's extended arm. As the truck would barely outrun them, down a hill, they would veer off into a ditch.

Kelvin wanted to get out of the truck, but there was nothing he could do but sit where he was. He patted the dog.

When they pulled into town, they bumped off the road and stopped at a gas station.

"I can take you a little farther after I fill up," the farmer said. Kelvin looked back at Roy Dean, jumping from the bed of the truck, empty now except for three melons still rolling around the bed. Kelvin didn't know what to say to the farmer so he didn't say anything. He got out of the cab and ran as fast as he could after Roy Dean, already lost up a side street.

They didn't stop running until they got to the schoolyard. They stood there panting, looking at each other. Roy Dean let out a tiny chuckle, then a louder one. Kelvin forced a kind of smile in the corners of his mouth and then he looked away toward the fields at the edge of town. Roy Dean suddenly laughed so loud that Kelvin jumped.

"You better get your daddy or somebody to drive you out and pick up the bikes," Roy Dean said. "They're gonna rust under those leaves." Then he saw something down the street that attracted his attention and he started walking in that direction.

When the two of them spoke after that, which was not often, they never mentioned the cantaloupes. More than he wanted to, though, Kelvin thought about the farmer, what he said to his wife when he got home. He guessed that Roy Dean was probably going to be an important man someday, because it didn't bother him at all. And everybody liked him.

Truth and Goodness

"Where—may I hope never to know—is Kelvin Fletcher?"

"Kelvin ain't here."

"Thank you, God." Homer Tuttle got his arms into the choir robe and popped the collar over his ears. "Everybody get in line. There goes the prelude. Get in line. Keep your hands out of sight. At least Kelvin's not here, maybe there won't anybody pick their nose."

Kelvin was running up the back steps of the church when he heard the music. He knew he was too late to get in line so he ran around to the front entrance of the sanctuary and sat in a pew before the choir had finished marching in. That was all right with him. He didn't like singing in the choir anymore anyway. Everybody knew he couldn't sing and old Mr. Tuttle kept making faces at him when he tried so all he did was move his lips with the words. If it wasn't that the Young People's Every-Other-Sunday-Night Choir had a hayride or a roller-skating party now and then, he would have quit a long time ago. So what if the movie he wasn't supposed to go to on Sunday ran long and made him late anyway?

Besides, now he could look at Salina Mae Becker for the whole hour. He had to think what he was going to do about her, because in six weeks he was going off to college and she was going to the junior college here in town. He knew that if he didn't do something pretty soon he never was going to do anything.

She was in the back row of the choir. It was elevated enough so he could see her from the breasts up. The white circle of collar made her look pure, so he always felt guilty when he thought about pulling the robe off of her. He didn't think about anything but sex when he looked at Salina Mae, but she was like an angel. It bothered him to have a hard-on when he looked at her in the choir robe. He looked away from her and caught the eye of Lettie Tuttle, Mr. Tuttle's daughter, who was in the middle row and too old to sing in the Youth Choir, but she did anyway. She was looking at Kelvin as if she knew something awful about him. He knew as soon as he caught her eyes that it was going to be a bad hour. He knew from a long time ago that when you catch someone's eyes in the choir you can't any more help looking at them again than you can help putting your tongue where a tooth was. He spent the first half of the service, until the sermon, looking back and forth from Salina Mae's breasts to Lettie Tuttle to the church bulletin in his hands.

After the sermon the choir sang "Amazing Grace," and Brother Cole gave the call to the altar but nobody came.

After church, outside where everybody was visiting and saying goodnight and the little kids were playing chase and rolling on the grass in their Sunday clothes, Kelvin asked Salina Mae if he could walk her home. She said "Sure."

They walked slowly and he told her why he was too late to get in line. He said that since he'd be going off to school in a few weeks he wouldn't bother about singing in the choir anymore anyway.

"Besides, Mr. Tuttle doesn't like me."

"He doesn't like anybody," Salina Mae said. He took her hand.

They walked more slowly still, talking about the movie he had seen and the last skate party and what a good guy Mr. Cole was for a preacher. They never got close to Salina Mae's house. After half an hour they were at the church again.

Kelvin thought it would be all right to lead her over to the dark part of the high front steps and sit down with her there, and it was. He decided to kiss her and she let him.

She kissed with her mouth open, which Kelvin was not used to. Then she put her tongue in his mouth. He got hard again and put his arm around her so he could touch her breast from the back. She took his hand and put it directly on her breast and he looked at it there.

"Do you want to go inside?" he said. Maybe she would and maybe she wouldn't but with just six weeks left he might as well find out.

"How can we get inside?" she said. "It's all locked up."

He tried all the basement windows on one side of the building and half of them on the other before he found one that wasn't locked. They crawled in and decided not to turn the light on. Kelvin kicked a toy duck or something that ding-donged all the way across the floor. He took Salina Mae's hand and led her upstairs.

"Do you know where we're going?"

"Yes," he said, lying.

"You find your way pretty good in the dark."

He didn't answer her. He didn't want her to think he had slipped into the church before but he didn't want her to know that it was his first time, either.

At the top of the stairs they turned left toward a dim light and saw that they were in the vestibule, where the ushers stand to hand out the bulletins. Kelvin could see a little from the street lights coming through the small front windows. He pushed open the great swinging doors of the sanctuary.

Light from the street lamps was falling through the one stained glass window directly over their heads. Purple, red, blue, green, and yellow over the pulpit and over the heavy carved preacher's chair. Kelvin led Salina Mae down the aisle, letting the doors close behind them. They walked holding hands toward the altar and all the colors. At first, when he had thought about going into the church, he was going to take her to the women's lounge, because there might be a day bed there and no window so they could turn the light on. It wouldn't be any good if he couldn't see her. But he didn't like the idea of making love in a ladies' toilet and that would be too much light anyway. Here there was just enough coming through the window, soft and colored and sort of romantic. There was a carpet behind the pulpit. They could lie on that.

So they lay down together. She helped him take her clothes off. He kissed her on her face and neck and her shoulders and finally her breasts. He leaned back to look at her and saw that she had a blue breast and a red breast and a face half green and half yellow. Her belly was purple. When she moved she changed like the colors in a kaleidoscope.

She was starting to undo his shirt.

"God," he said. "I don't have anything."

"You're kidding."

"I don't. I didn't . . . well, look, do we have to?"

"Yes, we have to!" she said. "What do you think?! For God's sake, Kelvin, do something! Kiss me!"

"I haven't got anything."

"Then get something, dammit! Go to the Gulf station. Don't they sell them there?"

"I guess so."

"You guess so?"

"Yes. They do. I'll be right back."

"Oh, Lord!" She was moaning as he got to his feet and started out. "This isn't happening to me!"

He tried to go through the window too fast and cracked his head. He fell back, sick at his stomach. Even before he felt with his fingers he could tell he was bleeding. He ran all the way to the gas station. He leaned against a tree and caught his breath so he wouldn't show he had been running when he asked for a rubber.

The clock in the station said ten. Nearly ten. He got a drink of water and studied a road map while a filthy man in overalls and another man in army clothes with the stripes torn off the shoulder drank Pepsis and talked with the man who ran the station. Kelvin was sure they weren't swallowing the Pepsis, just lifting the bottles and lowering them again. The bottles weren't getting any emptier. Maybe the men were spitting in the bottles.

He tried to think of some way to get them to leave. He thought of going out and setting their pickup on fire. He thought of Salina Mae.

"Whatcha need, son?" The manager moved a greasy rag over the glass-top counter. Inside the counter was stuff that looked like it hadn't been touched in a long time, Wrigley's Doublemint Chewing Gum and Clark Bars and pocket combs. Kelvin almost decided to buy a package of gum and leave but he couldn't go back to Salina Mae and give her a stick of gum. He thought he might get a ride in the pickup as far as the men were going and then keep walking until Salina Mae forgot about him.

"I need one of them rubbers you got back there," he said, trying to sound as much as possible like he might have come here also in the pickup truck.

The two men, the fat one and the one in the old army clothes, turned to look but they didn't say anything. The manager hit NO SALE on the cash register. He took a Coin-Pac out of the drawer and tossed it on the counter.

"Fifty cents," he said.

"Oh, my God."

"You're kidding," the station manager said.

"I got a problem."

"Looks like it," the man said.

"How many rubbers are there in that package? Could I buy just one?"

"There's just one in there," the manager said. "Maybe you'd like to buy just a piece of it." The men laughed.

"Aw-w-w, Goose," the fat man said. "Let him have it. He needs it worse'n you do."

"I ain't running no Salvation Army."

The filthy man pulled a quarter from his pocket and slid it across the counter.

"You get a move on, son. Do it good, now, you hear?"

"Much obliged," Kelvin said. He ran out the door, pushing the Coin-Pac into his back pocket.

"Hey," the man in the old army clothes yelled after him. "Don't that buy us a ticket?"

"Yeah," the other man said. "That ought to buy us a ticket."

Before Kelvin had run a block he heard the pickup starting. When he turned down the alley to the basement window he saw lights coming behind him. He ran up the alley on the other side of the street and dived into a clump of bushes. A branch scratched him across the cheek. He lay still while the pickup slowed down. He heard the men laughing as the pickup moved on.

. . .

Salina Mae was curled up in the big wooden preacher's chair, naked except for the cloth off the communion table which she had taken to wrap around her. She was nearly asleep. She didn't seem to think he had been gone for a long time.

"Hi."

"Hi," she said. She uncurled herself and helped him get undressed. They lay down together. He kissed her on the mouth and put a hand on her left breast as if he wanted to keep it from falling off.

"Honey," she said, "this rug is scratchy."

"Well, here." He got the communion cloth off the chair and spread it out for her. "Is that better?"

"That's fine," she said. "Kiss me."

He kissed her in her elbows. He kissed her knees. He said "I love you, I love you."

"I know," she said. "I know." She took his thing in her hand and pulled it toward her. He lay half on his side and started to move himself against her legs. She ran her hands over his body. She threw her head around so her hair went all over the red, purple, green, blue, and yellow of the communion cloth.

"What's that?" he whispered. "I heard something."

"What is it? I don't hear anything."

"Well, I heard something. There's somebody here."

"Why should anybody be in the church?"

"I don't know." He thought about the men in the pickup truck.

"It's outside," she said. "What's the matter with you?"

"Maybe somebody's breaking in." He was reaching for his underwear.

"Good Lord, Kelvin! Come on. I don't care if it's the devil. What are you doing?"

"It's not the devil I'm afraid of."

"Who then?"

"Nobody."

"Then would you please make love to me?"

He fumbled with the Coin-Pac and took out the rubber. He tried to unroll it over the limp flesh in his hand.

"I'm sorry. I've got to start all over again."

"Well, start!"

She slobbered kisses over his face and got above him so that her nipples dragged across his face. The rubber finally went on tight and he got on top and slipped inside of her.

He said to himself *I'm doing it with Salina Mae Becker.*

"Yes," she said. "Yes."

"Wow," he said, "Oh, wow!" and moved faster to make her happy so she would want to do it again even though he knew that any second the two men from the pickup truck were going to come in and kill him and finish off with Salina Mae. Or maybe they would sit down in the front pew and watch.

"Did you get through?"

"It doesn't matter," she said. "It's OK."

"Is it? Is it OK?"

"It's fine."

"Salina Mae, does this mean that we're going steady now?"

"Sure," she said. "Why not?"

"Listen, I got to have a picture of you, right? And I'll get you one of me, too."

"OK. Why not? Sure." She gave him a kiss and slipped out from under him. "That'll be great." They put on their clothes and didn't speak again until they were out of the church.

Before they got to the streetlamp she stopped and straightened her clothes.

"What do you think it was we heard in there?"

"I don't know what you're talking about, Kelvin. I didn't hear anything. Maybe God was trying to tell you something. That's his house you busted into."

"Could've been your daddy come looking for you," he said.

"Which would you rather?"

"I guess it wouldn't make much difference."

"Come on," she said. "I got to get in before ten-thirty. What time is it?"

"About that, I guess. I don't know."

"Let's walk faster."

In front of her house he kissed her twice.

"Are we still going steady?"

"Why not?" she said, and went inside.

In bed, he wondered if people had been making love in the church all the time and if everybody knew about it but him and the preacher.

He wanted to masturbate and he was disappointed because he thought after it happened that he would never want to masturbate again. He decided it was just habit and went to sleep.

During the next weeks they were used to each other and were easy being together and Kelvin knew that he knew what love was. They went swimming and on a hayride once. They stayed away from the church and they kept their secrets. They went to movies and took walks. They didn't make love again but they kept planning to when they could find a place, maybe when her parents were out of town and they could go to her house.

"I'm happier than I've ever been in my life," he told her one evening when they were sitting on the steps of her front porch.

"I know you are," she said. "I'm glad." It wasn't exactly what he wanted her to say.

"I love to kiss your nipples," he said one evening when they were sitting in swings in the playground of the grade school.

"I know," she said.

That wasn't what he wanted her to say, either.

"I leave for college tomorrow," he said one evening when they were sitting in the grass behind the high school gymnasium and she was putting her bra back on after they had touched a while. He wanted to look her in the eyes but couldn't help looking at the swinging movements of her breasts. "Are we still going steady?"

She grinned as if she didn't mean to.

"Of course we are." She pushed him off balance and fell on top of him. "Forever and ever."

She bit his ear and stood up, smoothing her skirt and brushing leaves from her blouse.

For a long time he didn't move, but lay still and watched her.

"Amen," he said.

He was always grateful to her but never forgave her. He was never alone with her again but she haunted his bedtime for years.

The Journal

Kelvin Fletcher took his new spiral notebook and turned it about so that the back became the front and then he printed JOURNAL across it in block letters, giving them a sculpted, three-dimensional look.

It was his third journal. For two months, since the beginning of the school year, one had been with him almost everywhere he went. He didn't keep the journal as a diary, but as a collection, bits and pieces of what he heard and saw as he went about his days. Once in a while he would try to tell something he had done, but he always gave up and marked out what he had written because as he put it down word by word it didn't seem as interesting as he remembered it.

One time he wrote down everything that was cut into the black rubber tabletop of one of the booths at Jack's Grill, the main campus

hangout, things like SMU   SUE   CALL 455–7822   KA SUCKS
MARIE DOTHAN DOES IT   GOD SEES ALL   FDR WAS HERE
4-1-41.

"That was April Fool's Day," Clement Long said in a sarcastic voice when he saw what Kelvin was writing.

"I know that, Clement."

Kelvin had never understood why Clement mostly seemed to be negative about everything. Like, this isn't true, this doesn't matter, we don't want to talk about that, why, no matter what you said he came back with an answer or a look that made you think you ought to have thought more about it.

"I'm going back to the room," Clement said. "Are you coming?"

"I don't guess so," Kelvin said, jiggling his can of beer to test its contents. "I guess I'll have another one. I want to think about something to write."

"I don't know why you keep a journal if you have to think of things to write in it. It seems like you'd keep a journal when you have more things happening than you can remember."

"People do things in their own ways."

"Right," Clement agreed. He gave Kelvin a soft slap on the shoulder and turned to go.

"I may not be around for a day or two," he said as he walked away, by which he meant that he would be staying over with that law professor friend that he talked with all the time and maybe even driving to St. Louis or Memphis for a concert or something without ever mentioning it but to say what he'd just said.

A girl Kelvin didn't know except that she was in his social science class came over to the booth and slipped onto the bench across from him. She said "Hi" as if they had planned to meet here and asked how his term paper was coming along. He knew it was Clement she wanted to talk about. Girls were everlastingly fascinated by Clement.

Most of the time, it seemed to Kelvin, they would hold back from Clement in public places, like they didn't want to show how interested they were, and whenever Clement wandered near a cluster of girls he was met with a flutter of nonchalance. Then they would sidle up and ask Kelvin about him. One time one of them wanted to know if Clement slept in his pajamas. Generally they asked if he had a girl at home.

Kelvin knew that Clement could have his way with most any of them and wondered why he didn't. Or if he did, maybe at the law professor's house. He had seen girls looking at Clement when he talked with a kind of captured look. They would look at Kelvin in nearly the same way when he talked about Clement. Now and then he would invent stories so they would keep looking, and he liked the way they smelled.

He would say that Clement had a beautiful girl at home, or that he was married before and his wife was killed in a train wreck, or that she was in an insane asylum. Once he told a girl that Clement made phone calls late at night in a language he had never heard.

...

One evening when Kelvin was walking home from the movies with Rosalie Powers, a sort of pretty girl with full lips and long, black, wavy hair with just a little dandruff who laughed too loud and used pretty bad language and whose daddy was some kind of preacher, she took hold of both his hands and pulled him off the sidewalk into the shadow of a tree. She leaned against the trunk and let go of his hands to push the hair from her face. They kissed and she raised a thigh to press it between his legs. There was a little popping sound from her chewing gum.

He led her down a hill toward the football stadium.

"Where are we going?"

"Just down here. We can go inside the concession stand."

"I don't want to do that. It's dirty in there."

"OK, then. Just here on the grass."

He spread his jacket on the dew, guided her to it, and sat beside it. He could feel the wetness coming through his clothes.

She let him run his hands across her blouse but told him not to get it wrinkled. She let him put his hand under her skirt when they had kissed some more. He tried to pull her skirt up but she pushed his hand down and told him not to get it wrinkled.

"How can I not get it wrinkled?"

"Take it off."

"Somebody might come by."

She sat up.

"Then let's go someplace else," she said.

"Where can we go?"

"What about your room, Kelvin?"

"I live in a dormitory," he told her.

"I know."

"They could send us back to the third grade."

"Not unless we got caught."

"Besides," he said, "I have a roommate."

"I know." She rolled away from him and sat up on her heels, kneeling, her hands in her lap.

"Are you afraid?" she asked him.

"Yes."

"Good. That makes it better."

. . .

       The room was dark. The sudden brightness from the single lamp Kelvin switched on was so intense it hurt his eyes. She took off her blouse and laid it carefully over the lampshade so that the room was suffused with a pale, lilac glow, then she turned toward Kelvin and waited. He kissed her, trying at the same time to slip a strap off one of her shoulders but it was too tight.

She moved out of his reach and dropped her skirt. She folded it and placed it on the dresser between the two beds. When she dropped her half-slip, Kelvin saw for the first time in his life a woman standing up in front of him in her underwear. This was like how it was if you were married. This was something to put in the journal.

She sat on the bed and he sat beside her.

They heard something in the hall. He froze.

"It's OK," she whispered. "The door's locked, isn't it?"

"Yeah, it's locked."

"Who has a key?"

"Just us. My roommate and me."

"So?"

She kissed him and he fumbled with the hooks on her bra strap.

"Are you going to keep your pants on?"

He stood to let the trousers fall to the floor. After he stepped out of them he seemed to freeze for a moment. Almost smiling, she took his head between her hands and turned it toward her face.

"Just get undressed, Kelvin. It's all right."

So he was naked, standing in front of her as she sat in her underwear on his bunk. She touched him and he was afraid he would embarrass himself in her hand.

"Wait," he said, and stepped back.

She stood up and reached her hands behind her back. He wanted to look into her eyes when she did this, to impress her, but he couldn't. The settling of her breasts when they were let loose from the brassiere seemed to him at that moment the most lovely motion he had ever beheld. Then she moved her hips quickly and she was naked, too.

After they had kissed and stroked each other a while, she took the gum out of her mouth and put it on the bedpost.

"Is this where you sleep?"

"Yeah."

She fiddled with him a little.

"Let's go over there."

"How come?"

She slid from Kelvin's bunk and took the two short steps to Clement's.

"Come on," she said, teasing.

When they were settled onto Clement's bedspread and pillow, touching along the whole length of their bodies, things were as complicated as he could stand them and he rolled to be on top of her, but she pulled back and took him in her hand.

"Wait a minute," he said.

"What?"

"I'm about to finish."

"Hey," she said. "It's OK."

...

She washed her hands at the sink, the only plumbing in the room, and they got dressed without talking. The hall was empty and they walked out as if they had lived there for years. Clouds hid the moon now and it was difficult to see. She took his hand.

They said goodnight at her dormitory door and she kissed him once.

"You probably don't even like me now," he said.

"Yes, I do, Kelvin. You may not believe it, but I'm still a virgin."

"Yes. I believe it."

He started to leave but she didn't let go of his hand.

"Listen," she said, turning him around to face her again. "It would have been great. This doesn't have anything to do with you."

"I know it doesn't," he said.

Back in his room, he sat up in bed until the ballpoint pen fell from his hand and the journal, the first page still blank, slid to the floor.

Coley's War

There were four of us. I'm Kelvin. The others were Coley and Monk and Paul. It doesn't seem now that we had very much in common but back then we kept ending up together, usually at Paul's cabin two-thirds up the side of Mount Carmel, a mile or so from the university. Actually it was his parents' vacation cabin, one of the summer places that cluttered the mountain, like the church camp I used to go to. Paul lived in it during the regular school year.

It was a good place to take girls or just to sit around and talk and drink beer. If anyone wanted to study he went to the library.

The porch faced west, where the foothills leveled out to flat farmland and the horizon was almost unbroken, like a view over the ocean. The sunsets were really something else.

From the moment the red sun began to flatten against the earth until it was gone, Coley would stand in silence, usually leaning against the wall of the cabin with the sole of one foot braced back against the stones that most all those houses are made of. He was not as tall as Monk, probably no taller than Paul, but he always seemed taller. For one thing, he was usually standing up and Monk and Paul were nearly always sitting down or lying back on the daybed or the couch or the bare pine floor.

Actually, I guess Coley would seem pretty average, just looking at him. Thin but not skinny, not especially handsome but a good face, brown hair that always looked like it needed cutting. It's his eyes I remember most. A sort of soft blue, not like they could see through you or anything. More like you could see through them.

Paul was the handsome one, if he hadn't always had a kind of sneer all the time. He looked like he might have come out of the movies, with hair so black it was almost blue and not a tooth out of line. He had a lot of expensive sport coats and he lifted weights. Still, he was always trying to please Coley. Coley made you want to please him.

Monk didn't have to lift weights. It was probably in his genes. He had a jaw so wide his face was square, especially with the crew cut he always wore. His chest was square, too. Even his feet were square. I was glad he was with us when we went to truck stop bars at the edge of town to talk to girls. Not that he looked mean. The fact is, his skin was almost pasty—just about the color of his straw-blonde hair. He thought of Coley as his best friend. I don't think Coley thought of Monk that way, but Coley didn't think of friends the way most people do.

One late September day we were sitting around on the porch talking, I guess it was just about sundown, when Paul said—he was sitting on the old banister—"You know something? If you fell over here and got the right bounce you could just about cram yourself down the chimney of Woodrow Wilson School or jam the steeple of the Baptist church up your ass."

"Jesus, Paul!" Monk said. "Why do you think about things like that?"

"The steeple would be better," Paul went on without a glance at Monk. "All the freshmen would have to salute you till your bones came loose. Then they could put them in a museum."

"Nobody's going to want your bones," Coley said from a redwood recliner, not opening his eyes.

"They might," I said. "Look at Matthew Brody. All he did was go off the Brooklyn Bridge, and he was real famous for that."

"He jumped," Coley said. "Nobody's going to want your bones unless you do it on purpose."

"Just listen to that!" Paul said to me. "You're probably the only person in the world that remembers his name. You probably remember the date. And what good does it do you?" He had a way of sticking both hands stiff-armed into his pockets when he was irritated. "You've got the lowest grades in the history of education and probably the best memory for junk. You're a friggin' idiot savant."

"Brady," Coley said. "It was Mathew Brady, not Brody!"

"Who cares?" Paul said, and went into the kitchen to get a beer. Monk was asleep.

That's the way we were. Friends, more or less. I think if you looked at us in those days, you'd say we were four guys without much of an idea about anything.

...

The first time I went up to the cabin was the day I met Paul. Coley introduced us at a sandwich place and left us there when he ran off to a class, so I offered Paul a ride home in the old Plymouth I had then. It barely made it up the mountain.

"Be at home," he said, and swung an arm toward the sofa. "Want a beer?"

"Sure."

He brought two from the kitchen and slumped into a big, over-padded leather chair on the other side of a low, round coffee table. On the shelf under the clear glass top there were all kinds of magazines, even *National Geographic*. I was impressed that he had them, but then I found out they belonged to his folks. I didn't think Paul ever read anything he wasn't going to be tested on.

We drank and talked until I had to go take a leak. Hanging from a string over the bathtub was a row of unrolled rubbers.

"What are you doing with all these things?" I called. "You collect rubbers?"

He came in and pulled the shower curtain shut. "Time for another beer. You want something stronger?"

"The beer can wait!" I said, following him into the living room. "You got to tell me what you do with those rubbers."

"No, I don't."

He got us each another beer and settled back into his chair. I stayed on my feet.

"You wash them?"

"What? You think I'm a slob? Of course I wash them."

"You use them more than once. I didn't know you could do that." I went back to my place on the sofa, not sure he wasn't pulling my leg.

"Once doesn't even break in a good rubber," he said.

"That's about the awfullest thing I ever heard of."

"You ain't heard much."

We took a couple of pulls on the beers. He wasn't grinning or anything.

"How come?" I asked.

"How come what?"

"Why do you do that?"

"Do what?"

"What are we talking about? The rubbers. How come you use them more than once?" For a second I was uneasy for having asked him, for having pushed the subject at all, for letting him know I'd seen them in the first place.

"Because I prefer to," he said.

"Well. How many times?"

"It depends." He could have been talking about an innertube or a guitar string. "After a while they get weak in spots. Excuse me." He unzipped his pants on the way to the bathroom. "I blow them up every week or so, when I remember. You can usually spot a weak place that way. Or it just breaks." He slid into the chair again and rested the still-sweating beer can on its fat arm. "The main thing is not to let one of the girls pop in and see them hanging there."

"I can see that."

"I mean, a girl really wants to think she's it, you know. But look, I don't want you to think I'm a pig or something. If I think a girl's a virgin, she gets a new one."

"Don't any of them do their stuff?" I asked.

"I don't trust them." He stood up as I pulled myself from the sofa and started toward the door.

"Thanks for the beer."

"I got a toothbrush in there that seven girls use and every one of them thinks it's just hers alone."

   . . .

           Monk was my partner in biology lab. I didn't think either one of us would get through the course.

"Is this a boy or a girl?" he asked, holding an enormous earthworm in front of his face, looking at it with phony earnestness. The lab instructor, a red-cheeked graduate student with a pencil in her hair, leaned over a dissecting pan at the next table and didn't answer him.

"Please, Teacher."

"You missed another lecture session, didn't you," she said, barely turning her head in our direction.

"I have to work sometimes."

"An earthworm is hermaphroditic. Do you know what that means?"

"Yes, ma'am."

"Good. I'm surprised." She straightened and left the room.

"It means it can go hump itself," he said for all the room to hear, and then collapsed in his own laughter. I sort of laughed, too. He was so big and loud that sometimes I was afraid of him.

. . .

I knew Coley best, or thought I did. Our sophomore year he asked me to spend Thanksgiving with his family in a small town in the hills on the other side of the state. I didn't have money to go home, anyway, living as far away from home as I did, so I said sure, why not, and we got out on the highway and started hitchhiking. It was about two hundred miles. I think we walked half of it, and half of that in the rain.

There's a moment, just before a rain breaks on you, when almost anyone will stop. And then, when the first drops fall, nobody will. We cut it too close. Nobody but a drunk lets you in his car once you're wet.

There wasn't any cover for miles, just cotton fields. Far off the road, set in the middle of the fields, were sharecropper cabins. Some of them looked empty, but they were impossible to get to, floating on mud. We came upon an old wagon at the edge of a field, but when we got under it we were still in a river of muck.

We came upon a small white building, a Zion African Methodist Episcopal church, and later a smaller cinderblock Freewill Baptist church, but they were both locked, doors and windows.

So we went on in the rain like it was sunshine, walking and kicking at stones. We saw a rabbit take off running, stop to listen, and then take off running again. We saw a calf standing alone under a tree, too far out in the field for us to join her.

I had the sniffles and my bones were cold. Cars whizzing by broke blades of water against our legs. Coley was talking to me about his family.

"I heard about Joe Hill," he said, "before I heard about Jesus . . . no, that's not true. But I heard about him more often." That impressed me, because I didn't know who Joe Hill was. "My father had old Sacco and Vanzetti clippings pasted in the back of Foxe's *Book of Martyrs*."

"I don't know what the *Book of Martyrs* is," I confessed.

"I'll show you," he said.

We finally made it to a Gulf station. It was already dark and the station was closed. There wasn't even a roof over the single pump so we spent the night sitting on the floor in the men's toilet. The toilet bowl didn't have a lid on it. The whole place smelled awful.

Coley woke me up before daylight.

"Come on," he said. "We got to get a move on before they open the station and find us here."

"What for?" I asked. "We're not doing anything."

"We know that," he said, "but they don't."

Just after daylight we caught a ride in a chicken truck. I slept. Sometimes I would half wake up and hear Coley and the driver talking.

. . .

Coley's father was a short man, broad in the shoulders. His round head was set under a mist of reddish hair. There was nothing about him to remind anyone of Coley, with his slender hips, his long, thin face, and the barely wavy brown hair he was always brushing back. Nothing, except a look that you can imagine John the Baptist might have had, a look that makes people likely to listen to you.

"Come in, son," was all he said to Coley. He turned to me and said, "Come in, come in," and stood aside, pushing the door wide. Coley gave his father a one-armed hug as he moved past to get hugged by his mother, then he turned and put both arms around his father's neck, and his mother hugged me like she had missed me all these years. She held me at arm's length and said, "My, my!" like she was surprised at how much I'd grown, then disappeared into another part of the house. Coley's father shook my hand and said, "We're glad you came."

In Coley's room we slept for most of the day. I opened my eyes to see a wide black leather belt hanging on the wall.

"What's that?" I asked him. "It could go around you twice."

"That's his. He used to whip me with it."

...

The next day we played ping-pong in the basement of the Methodist church and ran into two girls that Coley used to know. One had kind of short brown hair and one had blonde hair in a ponytail. We played doubles for awhile and then we all went to a place on the edge of town for beer. There was a guy there who Coley used to play baseball with in high school. He told jokes and the girls listened. He wore a cap that said Webb's Wrecker Service. The blonde was sitting next to Coley and when she laughed at one of the jokes she would drop her hand on Coley's leg. The boy would laugh, too, and push the bill of his cap up with his index finger until he was through laughing and then pull the cap forward again until the bill nearly hid his eyes. Then he would start another joke.

"They was this man invented a machine that got rid of niggers. He decided to see if he couldn't sell it to the Ku Klux Klan. He got it all set up, see, and the Imperial Wizard and everybody comes in and there's this machine with these two spics, one on each side of it, and the Wizard says, 'What's them spics for?' and the man says, 'Well ever once in a while you have to grease the machine.'" The girls laughed and the boy stomped his feet and spilled his beer.

"Aw, man . . ." Coley said, "that's not funny." He scooted his chair back.

The girl who was putting her hand on his leg looked around to see where he was going.

"It's funnier than any joke *you* know."

It was pretty quiet around the table then. The guy went over and started playing the pinball machine. I didn't know what to say to the girls so I went out the front door. There Coley was, sitting on the fender of a Ford.

"How come you left?" I asked him.

All the way back to his house, he didn't answer me.

...

I met Coley for the first time when we were freshmen. The second semester we started rooming together. We were both taking a sociology course taught by a man with a little head on a stalk that looked like a turkey neck. We had to write a paper. Most of us wrote on our grandfathers or running a paper route or doing a class play or something. You can make sociology out of anything. Coley wrote on U.S. and Latin American relations over the last twenty years. He must have read ten books.

On the other side of town from the campus, where the Missouri-Pacific cut through, there was a hamburger and beer place called Jack's. The booths were high-backed so you were almost in a room to yourself, the beer was cold, and half the records on the jukebox were country. Some of us used to go there one or two nights a week, get a pitcher, punch in some songs, and talk about whatever came up. Once, for at least half an hour it was Coley's paper we talked about because he wouldn't let go of it. Whenever he got serious his eyes would turn into slits, and while he was talking he would dig into the black rubber tabletop with a fingernail.

"Look, our whole sorry history with Latin America is a shame . . . So what? The world's a shame . . . Don't give me that . . . Give me a beer . . . Who's got the matches? . . . Some countries are not ready . . . That's not the point . . . Jesus, will you look at what came in? . . . Emiliano Zapata . . . Right, and remember Chapultepec . . . How can I remember it? I never heard of it . . . She's sitting by herself . . . *Hey, good lookin', what you got cookin'* . . . You sound like a communist . . . You wouldn't know a communist if you saw one . . . Who's got the matches? . . . We need some more beer . . . How do you know so much? . . . *Take these chains from my heart and set me free* . . . The whole place was settled by Catholics . . . You think those are real? . . . Where do you get all this political crap . . . Uh-oh, she's leaving, it's too late . . . My god, look at the way she walks . . . There's your politics, man . . . Hey, I'll vote for that . . . *I'm so lonesome I could cry* . . . Who has some money? . . ." and on and on like that as long as there was money for beer and the jukebox.

. . .

That's who we were. And this is how it began. We were sitting around the cabin the way we did most Sunday mornings, because none of us went to church. Monk didn't because he couldn't get moving on the weekend. Paul didn't because all they wanted was money. Coley didn't because he wasn't a Christian. I didn't because they didn't.

Coley was still into his Latin American thing. It had pretty near worked itself into an obsession. Sometime back he'd started to talk about going down there, actually going down there and taking up arms and fighting in this big revolution. We just let him talk. Now he was sounding serious. I didn't know how he could see, his eyes were such tight little slits. We'd heard of people who had gone down there where the revolution was going on, but they were all teachers or students at eastern schools. Most people we knew didn't care that much about politics of any kind, much less in some other country. The papers a few days before had told about an American student living in a guerilla camp, but his own brother said he was a radical. I wouldn't say Coley was a radical.

A few days earlier, Coley had gone to a poetry reading held to raise money for those same guerillas. The next day he drew his money out of the bank and gave everything he had to a man he met at the reading. We got very upset about that. Monk lifted a foot and farted the way he did when he thought somebody had done a dumb thing. Paul started peeling the label off his beer bottle.

"You don't want to get messed up in all that," he said to Coley. "You'd be so scared the first time you heard a shot your balls would fall off."

"Probably," Coley said.

It was October. The mountains were just getting the colors they keep until the first snow. They seemed close, like you could walk around them before supper. Late sunlight was lying across them with about half an hour to go, and the night birds were starting up. Monk was lying on a blanket he'd spread on the floor and looked asleep. I put my beer down and lay back on the lumpy cushions of a shaky wicker settee. I tried to sleep but Coley's voice was still going. It was hard to disagree with him. You wanted him to like you, to approve of what you were. You didn't want him to call you a coward. Not that he would.

"It's all set up," he said. "I might not get another chance. I don't see why it's so hard to understand. This is the Lincoln Brigade of our generation."

"What's that?" Monk asked.

"The Civil War, dummy," Paul said.

"Yeah, but not our civil war," I said. "The Lincoln Brigade was all the Americans that went to fight against Franco in the civil war in Spain."

"You're some kind of freak, you know that?" Paul said. "How come you're flunking out of school?"

"Coley," I said. "The Lincoln Brigade had more than one person in it. And they lost."

"Maybe all of us ought to go," Monk said. "You got to start living sometime."

"Life begins at conception and ends at birth," Paul said.

"Bring some beer when you come back," Paul called to Coley, who had gone into the bathroom.

"I'm meeting the others in Mexico next week," Coley said when he came out. "It's all worked out. It's just a matter of getting down there."

"Wait a minute," Paul said. "You don't even know this man."

"He knows Martinez."

"How do you know that?"

"I believe him."

"I guess you must. He has your tuition money for the next three semesters."

"I won't need it."

"How you going to find him?" I wanted to know.

"Easy," Paul said. "He'll be the man at the bus station with the automatic rifle and the red carnation."

"Make a joke of it," Coley snapped. "It doesn't make any difference now."

"Listen to yourself, Coley," Paul said. "You talk like you're in *Casablanca* or something."

Coley had a way of drawing his shoulders in and carrying his elbows close to his ribs, like a bird in the rain. It made him look smaller than he was. His voice sounded quiet no matter how upset he was, but you could always make it out in a roomful of people. There was no point in trying to go to sleep.

Monk got up to go to the bathroom.

"I think all of us ought to go," he said. "If Coley thinks it's such a big thing to do, I mean, why not?"

Monk kept his hair cut short, like a Marine. Part of his left earlobe was gone. He said it was bitten off.

"This is no party," Coley said. "People are getting killed down there."

"So how you getting to Mexico?" Paul asked him.

"Hitchhike, I guess."

"You have a car, Paul." Monk spoke on his way back from the bathroom.

Paul looked around at everybody and chewed on his lower lip for a second. "I guess I could drive you to the border. If you're really serious."

"Come on," Monk said, hitting fist to palm. "Let's do it!"

"I can't deny I'd appreciate the ride," Coley said. "Just to the border."

"Maybe," Monk corrected him. "Maybe not. We may decide to go all the way." He got off the blanket again and went into the kitchen. I heard the refrigerator click open. "Where's the beer?"

The sun was nearly gone. Coley turned to look south over the mountains.

"I would truly appreciate the ride," he said. "You do what you want to do."

"Well?" Monk said, mostly to Paul but partly to me. "Are you in or out?"

"Of what?" I asked.

"Who knows?"

"I don't know, man," I said. "What if we get down there and somebody starts shooting. I ain't never been shot at."

"A lot of those folks don't like Americans to begin with," Paul added.

"And with good cause," Coley said.

"You could probably get in a lot of trouble," I went on. "You could end up in prison or something."

Coley looked like I was boring him. Paul was grinning.

"You're the first real sissy I've ever liked," Monk said.

"OK," I said. "Why not? I'm flunking everything anyway."

"Right," somebody said.

"No matter," Paul said. "We'll all be back in two weeks. Say you were sick."

"I *am* sick," I said.

"Say anything you want to when you get back," Coley added. "For now, if you're serious, nobody says anything."

"Hey, listen," Paul said. "I'd take a blood oath, only I went and traded off my Captain America jack knife."

"What for?" Monk asked. He liked to play the straight man.

"Jobelle Simmons let me look at her left tit."

"She didn't let you look at both of them?"

"I only had one knife," Paul said.

...

Coley and I liked to play billiards. Not pool. Paul and Monk shot pocket pool. There was only one billiards table in town, in the back room of one of the pool halls, but nobody else ever played on it so Coley and I had it all to ourselves. Sometimes on a Saturday we'd start at noon and play almost till midnight. I was the second-best player in town. That was where we did most of our talking, and one reason we were closer to each other than to the others. I guess there were a lot of reasons for that.

Mostly I listened.

"Martinez is a lot like Emiliano Zapata," he said to me one day, stretching over the rail of the table.

"Look what happened to Zapata," I said.

"So what?"

The sound of a cue ball kissing one ball and then the other is consoling, exhilarating.

"Coley, what do you want to do if you go down there? Do you want to die or kill somebody or what?"

"I don't know."

"Then why do you want to go?"

He didn't answer for a couple of shots and I thought we were going to let it drop, so I changed the subject.

"You want to take in a movie?"

"Because," he began slowly, like he was talking to himself, "Martinez is a truly great man. I want to stand close to greatness."

...

An exchange student named Carlos had come from down there before the revolution started. Now he couldn't go home. He used to talk about the country, how beautiful it was, the mountains and rivers and all. He taught Coley a folk song, and Coley took him home with him over the Christmas holidays. They would speak Spanish together, partly so Coley could practice but partly so Coley could be different from us.

Carlos laughed a lot and swore by saints. And he liked to talk about Martinez, the liberator, who was in the hills and would someday come down. He wouldn't talk about the dictator, except to call him a son of a bitch and spit.

Then Martinez and his followers did come down from the hills. A week after the newspapers started carrying reports of the fighting, Carlos just about stopped talking. Coley said to leave him alone.

We'd gripe and be smartasses with Coley, especially when he got too serious, but sooner or later we would go along with what he said.

I don't know if he always was right, but he always sounded right. So we left Carlos alone.

Coley and Carlos would go out at night. I saw them a couple of times. I didn't try to join them. I figured they were probably speaking Spanish, anyway. Even if they weren't, I wasn't sure I would understand them.

We decided to go as far as New Orleans. It was a little out of the way but Paul said he wanted to go to New Orleans and it was his car. Monk and I liked the idea. Coley didn't seem to care. None of us had been to New Orleans except for Paul, who went every year to Mardi Gras.

Carlos showed up at the cabin early on the morning of the day we were going to leave. He and Coley took a walk around the mountain. They were gone for a long time.

Walking back to our room later that day from the last class of the term, Coley turned abruptly to cross the street into the playground of Woodrow Wilson Elementary School. I followed him, as a matter of course, to a set of swings. It was four-thirty; the kids had gone home. We sat in the swings and pushed ourselves back and forth without lifting our feet from the ground. Except for the creaking of the chains and the cars going by we sat in silence. Coley seemed to be thinking, but if I waited until he looked like he wasn't thinking I'd never speak to him.

"What did Carlos tell you?"

. . .

        We drove south, listening to country music and rock and gospel and sermons as we left the range of one small-town station and found another, searching the dial each time for the strongest signal. Sometimes we tried to sing along with the radio.

Coley and I could join in on most of the hymns and country songs. Paul and Monk knew the rock words when there were any. You could almost pat your foot to the rhythms of the preachers. Some were broadcasting from studios but some were coming from their churches, and the choirs would sing. Most of the sermons were awful but the choirs were wonderful.

We were southeast of Little Rock on 65, heading for Pine Bluff. Sister Mary Faith Hope of the First Church of the Early Warning told us to "beware-uh of-uh false-uh prophecies-uh," and someone else prayed for the Jews. We were getting close to Natchez when we heard about the lady PhD who found out that the little bodies of aborted babies were being used to make shampoo and hair cream. All the preachers wanted money.

We spent the night at a motel in Natchez. Paul put it on his credit card. We got to New Orleans about noon on Monday and checked into a motel in the French Quarter.

"I'll pay you back when I can," I told Paul as he slipped the credit card back into his wallet with all the others.

"Don't worry about it," he said. "Just let me use your wife on your wedding night."

"You're not going to lay a debt on *me*," Coley said. "It was your idea to come along."

"I didn't say anything about a debt," Paul said.

"He didn't say nothing," Monk said.

. . .

That night we had dinner at what I thought was a fancy restaurant, but it wasn't one that Paul said he'd have liked to take us to—we didn't bring the right clothes. He was the only one with a tie and Monk's only jacket was one that zipped up.

After we ate Paul took us around to some places where we listened to jazz. I liked that almost as much as the preachers. We didn't stay long at any one place because Coley sat like he was deaf and Monk got nervous. We ended up at a little room called Preservation Hall that was my favorite, but Paul didn't care as much for it. He said it was primitive jazz and he wasn't surprised that I liked it. I can still hear it.

After that we walked up and down Bourbon Street looking in the places where there were strippers. The men standing out front would hold the doors open for a couple of minutes and holler at us to come in because there was no cover charge, or if we were close enough they would say it in a confidential voice like they were trying to talk us into joining a church. If we stood there without starting in they would close the doors.

···

We took a bottle back to the motel and drank and talked till we fell asleep. Mostly, Monk and Paul told jokes. Next day we slept till noon. As we drove out of town toward Texas I asked Paul if we had seen New Orleans.

"All I know of it," he grumbled. He was pretty hung over. Monk was already asleep beside me in the back seat. Coley was driving.

We stopped once when Paul thought he was going to throw up, but except for that and a stop for gas we drove straight through into Texas without a break and with hardly a word spoken.

···

"It won't hurt you to take a drive into Mexico," I said to Paul and Monk, mainly because I wanted to go myself. We were parked at the border guard station. We could see the Mexicans across the border in their uniforms, which were wrinkled like they'd been slept in. The American guards looked like they were ready for a class picture. And the Americans' official vehicles were regular cars; the Mexicans had two dark green military vehicles parked in front of their guardhouse. They slouched with rifles and talked and laughed, then looked almost surly. The Americans, unarmed, looked bored. Across the highway from the Mexican guardhouse a score of people sat or squatted on the ground.

"I never been in another country," Monk said. "I don't have a passport."

"You don't have to have a passport to go to Mexico," I said.

"They let you go thirty miles," Coley said.

There were a bunch of soldiers, it looked like mostly officers, and maybe a dozen small boys, a few girls the same age, a skin-and-bones woman, some old men, and a tough-looking boy of maybe seventeen. Coley spoke to the officers in Spanish. He told them we were students come to practice our Spanish.

. . .

We had a map Coley had marked with a felt-tip pen to outline a winding route far off the main highway. I didn't see a town anywhere along the route, but Coley said we'd find it where the road turned south and the mountains rose just ahead of us. That was what Carlos had said.

"Jesus Christ, Coley," Paul said. "I wish you could hear how dumb that sounds. Like we're spies or something. Why didn't we just take a plane down and skip over Mexico?"

"The airports are controlled by the government," Coley said. "We are not on the side of the government."

"We are not on anybody's side," Paul said. "We get that close, this boy is going home."

"This one, too," Monk said. "I ain't mad at nobody. If I was, I'd raise a stink, but I ain't."

They're right, I thought. Nothing's happened. We can always go back.

Paul, who had been to Mexico many times, said we oughtn't to travel at night because there were donkey carts, trucks, and buses with no lights.

"Good idea," Coley said. "We don't want to get involved in an accident and have the police come across the gun."

"The what?" I said. "You got a gun?"

"What do you think I'm doing here?"

"I don't know. Nobody said anything about guns. Fact is, I don't know what any of us is doing here."

"Nobody made you come," he reminded me. "You can turn around whenever you want to."

"Right," I said.

. . .

The first three nights we pulled off the road and slept on the ground between blankets. Paul bitched constantly. Monk said it wasn't nothing. By nightfall of the fourth day we were in a little town called San Pedro, far off the main highway, where sure enough the road finally turned due south and we could see the mountains directly ahead. That's where we had our first trouble and lost Paul.

...

Coley knew enough Spanish to get us a couple of rooms for the night in the only two-story building in town, a stucco hotel with about four rooms. It had cracks in the walls almost wide enough to put my hand in and one toilet, which was at the end of the hall on the second floor. Paul said he wanted to go out and practice the little Spanish he knew. Paul always had money to spend. The rest of us went to bed. About eleven o'clock Paul came in. He sat on the dresser and put his feet on the metal bed I was sharing with Coley. That woke me up. In the light of the single bulb, his shoes were untied and he was grinning whole sentences.

"What?" I said, trying to shake the sleep out of my head.

"You ain't gonna believe this," Paul whispered.

"What?" I didn't want to wake Coley.

"You want to have some adventure? Get your clothes on."

"I don't think we ought to wake Coley up."

"Then don't." He slid off the dresser and started for the door. I lay back on the musty pillow as the door opened and Monk came in in his undershorts. He looked sideways at Paul.

"You been out whorin' around, ain't you?" Monk said.

Paul shrugged.

"Tell me."

"Get your clothes on and I'll show you."

There were three cantinas in the town, small, dim rooms with planks laid across barrels for bars and rows of hotcakes and Pepsis on shelves, in addition to the beers, which were the only thing kept cold. They had two or three tables and a few rickety chairs. Wherever we went the talking stopped. We found her in the second cantina.

Paul spoke to her and bought two bottles of tequila. She left two steps behind him and we followed. The two other customers and the man behind the bar paid us no mind. The woman looked back at me and smiled. I thought she was almost pretty. She was dark with long hair. Long, long, black hair. I didn't know what was going to be expected of me.

It was a clear night. A warm breeze blew over us. We walked from the village square to a little two-room clay house with a ceiling that barely let Monk stand up without bending over.

The front door was a sheet of plywood. It couldn't close all the way. The woman lit a kerosene lamp that spread a whiteness about the room, and then she took off her blouse. She didn't wear anything underneath it. I had an erection right off and I thought I might come in my pants before anything happened. Then she dropped her skirt and she didn't have anything on under it, either.

All this wasn't like she was doing a striptease or anything. It was just like what it was—she was taking her clothes off. Then she put the lantern on the hard dirt floor. Her breasts shook when she walked.

Then a smell hit me, wine and kerosene, sweat and old bedclothes, chickens, and something dug up out of the ground. Paul opened a bottle and took a drink. The woman walked over to him and took the bottle. From across the room she brought a knife and a lemon and a salt shaker. She cut the lemon in two and showed us how to drink tequila. We did what she did and watched her nipples jerk and tremble until we were all aglow and out of our clothes.

She put the bottle out of the way and sat on the edge of the empty table and leaned back on her thin brown arms. She looked at each one of us in turn. When she looked at me she smiled like a puppeteer and pulled a string and let it go.

Monk got up first and stepped into the space she made between her knees, but when he started to take her thighs in his big hands she wiggled loose and off the table. He fell back and had to steady himself.

She walked a quick circle around us, nearly dancing. She slapped her hair across Monk's face and reached down to flip my prick. She smiled that terrible quick smile again. My head was beginning to float above my shoulders.

Then she went slowly to her knees in front of me and took me in her mouth. I could barely feel her teeth. I was embarrassed that Monk and Paul saw me when I came.

She spat on the dirt floor and walked on her knees to Paul.

"El dinero, señor."

"She wants her money," Paul said. "This was just a preview."

"Give it to her!" Monk said. "Give her the money."

Paul lifted his pants off a chair, took a bill from them and gave it to her. She looked expectantly at Monk and me.

"What?" Monk said.

"Everybody pays," Paul said, and laughed. "You think I'm gonna buy you that?"

Monk got his pants and gave her a bill. So did I.

"What you paying for?" Monk snorted. "You already got yours."

"It's a debt of honor," I said, trying to make it sound like a joke.

She lay down on the narrow cot. Monk got on her and the cot broke. I think she hurt her head when she fell. We took turns sucking her tits and kissing her and screwing her. Then the kid walked in.

"Mamá. Qué haces, Mamá?"

. . .

I guess he was about five. He was naked, standing in the blanketed doorway with his little dick sticking straight out toward the three-headed, twelve-limbed animal eating his mother. She said something to him but he didn't move.

I asked Paul what she said.

"I don't know," he answered, shouting. "I don't know. I don't understand this fuckin' language."

"Qué haces, Mamá?"

He was starting to cry. She yelled and threw somebody's shoe at him. He ran out the front door of the house.

Monk, between the woman's legs, pitched his head forward and vomited on all of us.

. . .

We used what little water she had and the rest of the tequila to wash ourselves off but she wanted to go back to the hotel with us and get it out of her hair. The kid was lying awake in a hammock at the side of the house. His mother covered him with a ragged and dirty old poncho and fell in behind us as we headed back to the main street.

The desk clerk at the hotel was as drunk as we were. He didn't see us go in or if he did he didn't care. The door to the small bathroom was shut and the sounds from inside told us to wait. We sat on the stairs until a fat woman in a flannel gown came out carrying a cat. Her streaky hair hung gray and red to her waist.

The shower was a three-sided sheet-metal stall straight across from the door, squeezed between the lavatory and the commode. Paul went to the room he shared with Monk to get soap and shampoo and towels. The woman took her clothes off and got in the stall. She stood there with the water off and signaled for me to get in with her. Monk was obviously too big. I took my clothes off and stepped in. She turned the water on without testing it and we both jumped out of the icy drizzle. She laughed.

When Paul got back naked from his room he found us in a warm rain, lathering each other with a sliver of soap somebody had left. Paul handed us the soap and shampoo and stood naked watching us while Monk used the toilet. She washed me all over. Paul took my place and she washed him. Monk was sick again.

The shower didn't do much to get us sober. We all went naked to Paul and Monk's room and Monk started playing with her again. She pushed him away and rubbed her fingertips against her thumb.

"She wants more money," Monk said.

"Hey," Paul sang. "You're learning the language."

"No more money from me," I said. "I've still got to eat."

"Eat that, man." Monk reared back and pointed to her bush.

He pulled two soggy dollars out of his jeans and handed them to the woman. She wrapped her hand around the bills and lay down on the bed. Monk crawled on top of her but he couldn't make anything happen. He raised himself on all fours above her and looked at Paul.

"I want my money back," he said. "Tell her I want my money back."

"Don't worry about it," Paul said. "I've got a better idea."

...

Paul and Monk put on dry clothes and I carried the woman's wet clothes and mine to the room where Coley was sleeping. Inside, we squatted between the bed and the window while the woman pulled the sheet off Coley and knelt on the mattress beside him. She spread his fly and lifted his prick into her fingers. He groaned like he was dreaming. We slunk down farther below the level of the bed. I started to feel ashamed.

She took him in her mouth and he opened his eyes. He closed his legs around her head and I watched him come. Then he saw us.

He rolled out of the bed so angry I thought he might break her neck. She fell to the floor and he looked for a moment like he was going to kick her. He yelled at us and then picked up his suitcase and threw it at us. He got the only chair in the room, a cane-bottomed straight chair, and banged it on the floor. I thought he was just showing his anger, but then I saw that he was trying to break a leg loose. Monk jumped over the bed and tried to take the chair away from him. Coley turned away without saying anything else and looked out the only window in the room, a dirty window with broken glass, while the woman put on the vomity clothes and left us without a word or a look. Then Coley spoke very softly without turning away from the window. He called us pigs and Yankees. Paul and Monk went back to their own beds.

I didn't know what to do or what to say. I suddenly realized that I was naked. I went to bed and pretended to close my eyes but through my lashes I could see Coley standing at the window, looking out at something I might not have seen even if I had been standing beside him. I wanted to tell him that I wasn't really a part of what had happened, but I was. I wanted to tell him that I wished it hadn't happened, but I wasn't absolutely sure. I turned over and shut my eyes against the bulb hanging from the ceiling. It had turned the world outside the window into a black mirror.

⋯

Nothing was said about it the next morning. I couldn't see even a pout on Coley's face. It wasn't that he was giving us the silent treatment or anything. It was like it just hadn't happened.

We locked our bags in the car in front of the hotel and walked across the road to the cantina where Paul had found the woman. The road was deep with red dust and we kicked up clouds of it. There was a musty smell I remembered from hot afternoons when I was a child, when it hadn't rained for weeks and the cotton was dying and the chickens and dogs stayed together under the house. We squinted against the sun and sucked in the hot air. Halfway across the road we heard a man shout.

"Gringos!"

I knew at that very moment that I was going to die there in the red dust in a town I didn't know the name of. I thought of my parents, who didn't even know where I was.

"Gringos!"

When I turned and tried to focus on him, the waves of heat and the sweat running into my eyes turned everything to a mirage. I wiped the sweat away with my sleeve and squinted at a man who was standing like he had been ordered to attention, maybe three or four storefronts down the road. His face was lost in the shadow of a straw hat. A dull serape hung from his shoulders. It covered his whole body, down to his feet.

"Desgraciados!"

He moved toward us stiffly, his arms hidden inside the serape. I think now how much he looked like a pawn on a chessboard, but I wasn't thinking that then. He took small, slow steps. The dust swirled around his ankles. He might have been walking through a field of reddish brown flowers that bloomed and died every time he took a step.

"What's the matter with *him*?" Monk asked nobody.

"You sons of bitches," Coley whispered.

"Let's get out of here," I said.

"Don't get your bowels in a panic," Paul said. "He won't do anything. What *can* he do?"

"What do you think?" Monk said. "He might have a gun."

I started back toward the car. Monk stopped me.

"Just take it easy. We can handle him. Four Americans, man. We ain't gonna run."

"You speak for yourself," I told him and started for the car again. He grabbed my shirt.

"Don't cut down the odds. Though God knows what good you'd be if there really was trouble."

About ten feet away the man stopped. The dust settled and I could see that he was barefoot. I could barely make out his eyes under the brim of his hat. Then he threw his arms up and the serape fell back over his shoulders like a cape. In his right hand there was a long knife. Monk pushed me aside, took three steps toward the man and kicked him in the stomach. The knife fell to the ground as the man doubled over. Monk stood there looking at him, waiting for him to get up. When he tried to, Monk kicked him again. Coley ran over and pushed Monk away.

"You don't have to kill him."

The Mexican pulled himself to his feet and hit Coley in the face as hard as I've ever seen anybody hit and then he hit Monk, who was standing there confused. Monk spit blood and knocked the man across the road. I saw a lump of serape lying in the dust with a hat still in the middle of it.

Two more Mexicans were coming cautiously toward us. Monk turned to face them, crouched down like a linebacker. Paul picked up the knife. I started again for the car, then I remembered that it was locked and I didn't have the key. The two other men were almost on us. There was a tall, skinny one and a fat one, like Laurel and Hardy. They looked mean. I was so scared I couldn't breathe.

"Put the knife down," Coley said through his bloody lips. He was still trying to get up.

"Not likely," Paul shot back, and squatted down with the knife pointed out in front of him like he knew what he was doing. Coley pulled himself to his feet and stumbled toward the two Mexicans. "Somos amigos."

The tall one swung his hand around with a rock in it and caught Coley on the side of the head almost exactly where the other man had hit him. He fell backward without even trying to catch himself. Monk grabbed the fat one and wrestled him to the ground. I started to run but I was afraid not to be with the others. I stopped to see if Coley could run and the tall man kicked me in the ribs. I fell on top of Coley. I think I started crying. I lifted my head to see if I was going to get kicked again and saw the first Mexican, the one in the serape, getting up. He moved like Frankenstein, in small, stiff steps. He was walking toward Paul. Paul was hopping around, still in a crouch, with the knife stuck out in front of him like a pistol, yelling. "You asked for it," he said. "Now you're gonna get it."

He started running toward the man, who was all serape and hat, still with no face. Paul jumped on him the way a small boy will go running and jump on his grandfather, weighing him down. He sat straddling the shape and I saw the knife come up over his head and fall and heard Paul cry out, "Ah-hee!" and then "Ah-ha."

For a long while everything froze and then a cloud of roaring dust like something from the *Wizard of Oz* came to a stop just where Coley was barely moving. The dust settled around a car the color of the dust. One of the front fenders was missing. Out stepped a bony, sort of good-looking man not much older than us, wearing a wrinkled khaki uniform with a badge and a policeman's cap. He stood with his hand on the open door.

"My town is your town," he said. I thought he started to smile.

. . .

The Chief, who had left his sprinkled, rusty Buick in the middle of the road where he had stopped the fight, followed us into the narrow door of the mud building with barred windows, keeping his hand on his holstered pistol all the way.

It was cool inside. I guess that was because of the thick mud walls. There were three small cells set in a row opposite the only door. Each cell had a cot and a slop jar. In the one on the left there was a skinny, very brown man of about twenty. There was a tall older man with gray hair in the middle cell and a dwarf in the cell on the right. The sheriff opened the middle door and apparently told the tall man to get into the cell with the dwarf, which he did. The four of us were signaled into the middle cell. All you could hear was breathing. The Mexicans on each side of us stared at us standing there with our arms folded or our hands in our pockets, looking anywhere but at each other.

"Which man of you put into the boy the knife?" The Chief was sitting on his desk, swinging his feet so his heels bumped against it. I was surprised to hear him refer to the man in the serape as a boy. *Clump-clump.*

"Which man?" *Clump-clump.* His face didn't show anything at all.

Coley grabbed the bars of the cell.

"Is he all right? Is he hurt bad?"

The sheriff shrugged. "He will die, of course." *Clump-clump.* His face didn't show anything at all.

Paul sat down on the cot.

Clump-clump.

"Hey gringo!" The voice came from the cell with the tall, gray-haired man and the dwarf. They were both sitting like clay figures, looking not exactly at us but rather toward us, with no more expression than the Chief showed. The dwarf was on the cot. The tall one was sitting on the floor, leaning against the cell wall with his hands behind his head.

"What are you doing here?" he asked in a flat voice.

"Look," Coley said, shifting his position to take hold of the bars that separated our cells, "maybe you can help us. I'm sorry about what happened out there."

Clump-clump.

"Listen," Coley tried again. "We're not what you think. We're down here . . . well . . ." Then he looked at the Chief. He didn't go on.

Monk was restless. He'd been standing at the small window in the wall behind us, shifting his weight from one foot to the other and cracking his knuckles. Now he turned around and pushed his fists down into his pockets.

"I want out of here," he said.

Clump-clump.

Paul sat on the cot and cleaned his fingernails with his thumbnails. "Which man?"

Monk lifted his leg and farted.

"Hey gringos," the Chief said a few minutes later. "How brave are you?"

"How brave is anybody?" Coley answered without looking at him.

"Not anybody, amigo. This is not for to be a philosopher. This is for you. Usted. How brave are you?"

"I don't know," Coley said. "How brave do I have to be?"

"Always the question for the question. I did not ask if you are so clever."

"I don't know," Coley said again. "I'm not sure I know what bravery is."

"That is strange for you to say. Today you saw it. You touched it, no?"

He slid off his desk and left us.

. . .

"What's all this?" Paul snapped as soon as the Chief had closed the door. Nobody spoke or moved.

"Coley, I asked you a question."

"I didn't know you were talking to me." Coley still didn't move.

"Now you know."

"So what do you mean?"

"Don't give me that. You know what I mean. What are we doing here in this stupid town? We could just die here, because you got us here, and it's not even on the way to where we're supposed to be going. We were just on a vacation, that's all."

"What *are* we doing here?" I asked. "It isn't even on the way, is it?"

"No," Coley admitted. "In a way, it's not."

"What do you mean, in a way?" Paul was sneering.

"It's not on a straight line, but there was a . . . well, a reason."

Then I knew.

"Carlos," I said. "He told you to come this way, didn't he?"

Coley nodded.

"Why would he want us to come here?" I asked in a whisper.

"I don't know," Coley said.

. . .

A couple of hours later we decided we might as well get some sleep. Monk was on the cot and the rest of us were curled and sprawled on the floor. Just as I drifted off I heard a voice that sounded like Coley.

"Why did you do it, Paul?"

"Go to sleep, man," Monk said. "It's gonna be OK. He don't know who did it."

"Anyhow," Paul said, "it was an accident."

"It wasn't an accident," Coley said.

"No," Monk agreed. "No accident. It was self-defense. It was him came with the knife, right?"

"Right," Paul grunted.

"That was his wife, you know." Coley bit off the words.

"So?" Paul said.

"It could have been his sister," Monk said. "Who gives a fuck?"

"He's dead," Coley said.

"I didn't mean to," I barely heard Paul say as I fell asleep.

. . .

I was awakened by Paul as first light was coming up on the objects in the room. He was grunting and swearing, trying to break a piece of mortar off where the wall met the floor. When he finally pulled it loose he tossed it at the head of the tall man, asleep on the floor in the next cell. It didn't rouse him. Paul asked me for another one. I worked a piece loose and handed it to him. He flicked it carefully and it hit the Mexican on the mouth.

He jerked awake and sat up. He felt around for what had disturbed him and picked up the chunk of mortar. I had an impulse to tell him I didn't throw it, but he was looking directly at Paul.

"Maybe if I go back to sleep you will throw me a dollar, eh, gringo?"

Paul hushed him with a finger and signaled him to come close. The three of us squatted near the bars.

"When do *you* get out of here?" Paul asked him.

"Very soon. Tomorrow. And tomorrow has already arrived. Why do you want to know?"

"You can help us."

"Why should I help you, gringo? I hate the smell of you."

"God," Paul said. He threw his hands up again and then jerked a thumb toward Coley. "You sound like him! I'm not interested in politics. I don't care whether you hate me or not. I want to pay you money to do something for me." They stared at each other. "A taxi driver doesn't have to like his passengers. You do something, you get paid for it. It's got nothing to do with politics."

The Mexican kept his eyes on Paul and ground his teeth.

"I want you to get in touch with my father."

"And if I do this?"

"A hundred dollars."

"This is what your life is worth?"

Paul's face screwed up.

"This is a great inconvenience to me."

"Death is a great inconvenience."

"Five hundred. Just make one phone call."

The Mexican scooted away from the bars and leaned against the cot where the dwarf lay sleeping.

"All right. A thousand. A thousand dollars."

"How do I know that you have a thousand dollars?"

"My father will bring it. You will see him before I do."

"Two thousand."

"Go to hell."

"As you wish."

"Two thousand dollars," Paul whispered. "So do it, then. I have the number here." He held a small piece of paper through the bars and dropped it.

"Very good. Now I will say something to you." The Mexican sat up Indian-style and stuck a straw in his mouth. "I leave today, but not to be free. I leave for the prison. So you can keep your money. And I will say something more. If they would let me go free today I would not call for your father to come. You make me sick."

"So go to hell," Paul snorted. Then he spat toward the Mexican but the spittle hit a bar and slid down it.

The Mexican grinned.

. . .

Next morning, after bread chunks and coffee, Paul told the Chief he wanted to make a phone call but he didn't get an answer, not even a look. Back on the mountain when we were sitting around sharing stories about some fool in a bar, we used to talk about sensing your own mortality. That was on my mind.

"Are you going to charge us with something?" Coley asked, not as a challenge, but like he wanted change for a dollar.

"Yeah," Monk put in. "What about a lawyer?"

"Shut up, Monk," Paul growled. "Everybody just shut up. They're not going to keep us in here." His face froze. He was staring at the Chief.

"You have good fortune," the sheriff said. "Many times the judge comes not so soon. Today he comes. Perhaps he find only one of you guilty." His broad grin showed dark, uneven teeth. He touched a finger to his hat and walked out into the bright dust of the street.

Coley spoke to the tall man.

"I don't know who you are, but you're obviously not a local . . . not a . . ."

"Campesino is a good word," the man said. "It's not like saying nigger."

"If you can help us get out of here . . . We have business to get to . . ."

"So do we all."

"We were on our way . . . trying to get on our way to help . . . Martinez."

Paul snarled at him. "You speak for yourself."

Coley ignored him.

"Sir, do you know who Martinez is?" Coley asked the tall man.

"He has nothing at all to do with Mexico. That is another country, far, far, to the south. Another world."

"It's all one world," Coley said, turning a full circle, shaking his open hands and then slapping them to his head like it might fall off.

"God," Paul said. "He's going to preach."

"How could I possibly help you?" the man asked. "We are all here in the same jail."

"I don't know," Coley sighed.

The tall man spoke again after a long silence.

"Why?"

Silence.

"Why?"

"Because of what he stands for."

"What does he stand for?"

Silence.

"You are here to help him because of what he stands for, but you cannot tell me what he stands for. See how silly you are. You talk silly. You think silly. You are a silly man."

"The people."

"And who are the people? The people are as silly as you are."

The tall, gray-haired man leaned back on his cot and chewed on a straw. The young man in the other cell looked like he understood nothing of what was being said. The dwarf lay on his side with one eye open. The tall man got up to look out the window.

"Yanqui go home!" the dwarf called out, and he laughed and pointed at us.

"Oh, my God!" Paul said. He dropped onto the cot and buried his face in his hands.

Then the Chief came back. There were two men with him. One wore a pistol and a crumpled brown uniform that was too large for him. The other had on slacks and a sports shirt.

"Pues, amigos," the tall man said. "I leave you."

His cell door was opened and he held out his arms for the cuffs the man in the slacks was rattling.

"Adiós," he said, raising his cuffed arms over his head and leading the way out of jail. The dwarf was given a signal to follow them, and he did. The skinny, young guy was let out, too. The Chief locked the door from the inside and sat again on his desk.

Clump-clump.

I was getting sick to my stomach.

"How much is it worth to you to go?" The Chief asked us all. "To the south or to the north, as you will, how much is it worth?"

We looked at each other. I shrugged my shoulders and sat down on the couch. Coley sighed and let his gaze drop. Monk said, "What kind of country is this?" and jabbed his fist in the air.

"I want to go home," Paul said.

"Five thousand dollars," said the Chief. "I will call your father."

"You're holding us for ransom, ain't you?" Monk sneered.

Paul signaled him to shut up.

"My father is not a rich man," Paul said.

"He had better be."

Eight hours later Paul's father was there, in his own plane, with the money. He was a very round man, with no hair anywhere to be seen, except for great black eyebrows.

. . .

"What's all this about?" he said as he walked into the jail. "What's going on here?" Paul told him about the fight, not about the woman.

"The boy is dead," the Chief announced for Paul's father's benefit.

"Jesus," Coley said. "I'm sorry."

"I advise you now to pay this fine and go before friends of the boy become more angry again."

Paul's father counted out the cash.

"This is for all four of them," he said.

"Por cierto," said the Chief. "I have no use for them."

"They can drive back," Paul's father announced crisply. It was not something to be discussed. We were given our belongings and Paul handed Coley the keys to the car. There was a small crowd around the jail as we left.

Paul's father was moving his head in little jerks.

"Would it not be a good idea for you to walk to the plane with us?" Paul's father asked the Chief, pushing a wadded bill into his hand. "These people may not understand that we have paid the fine."

"You will not be hurt," the Chief said. He put the bill in his pocket and closed the jail door behind us, standing with us in the hot air. I nearly wished I was inside again.

We shook hands with Paul and watched as he and his father and the Chief walked up the road to the north edge of town, where the pilot stood beside a blue and silver Cessna. Paul turned back to speak to us as he walked.

"Bring the car back, Coley."

Monk and Coley and I hurried off in the opposite direction. The Mexicans let us pass but you could almost hear them staring. I wanted to run but I was afraid it would start them running after me. A group of ten or twelve men followed us to Paul's car. Sitting in the front seat of the car was the tall, gray-haired man from the jail. He spoke to Coley in even better English than he had used before.

"I'll take you the rest of the way. Please get in quickly."

I knew then that we were not going home. We couldn't stay here, so Monk and I got in the back seat. Coley slipped behind the wheel. As we began to move a rock hit the back window. Then one hit the trunk. I turned around to see a dozen men running after us, their legs lost in roiling red dust, waving their arms and shouting. In a few seconds they were like a mirage in the distance, a vague motion against the dusty buildings.

· · ·

"You should have gone back with Paul," Coley said to Monk and me.

Neither of us said anything. He was right.

We rode in silence then for maybe five minutes. Not even Monk asked what was going on. The desert was spread out on each side of us toward mountains that might have been five or fifty miles away. Then the Mexican spoke.

"You did not make things very easy for us."

"Us who?" Coley asked him.

"Who do you think?"

"Is all this going to be explained to us?"

"In time," the man said.

We were obviously in the hands of a Martinez man. I didn't know if that was something to be glad about or not, but at least we were not in jail.

As we moved through the countryside the man directed Coley to take this or that road.

"I'm sorry the boy died," Coley said.

"He did not die."

"He didn't?"

"No."

Again we rode in silence.

"The Chief was lying?" Coley said.

"Yes."

The man reached down and pulled a bag from between his feet, a leather satchel like an old-time doctor's bag. He handed it back to me. It was filled with American money.

"Five thousand dollars can be very useful," he said.

We rode in silence for long, dusty miles.

"The Chief is one of you?" Coley said.

"It would seem so," the man said.

Monk and I sat in the back seat with nothing to say. It was pretty clear we had passed the place where we could turn back. Monk slumped in the seat, scowling as if he'd flunked another test.

Coley talked without taking his eyes off the road.

"You were waiting for us," he said for the record. "Carlos set all this up."

"Not all of it," the Mexican said. He shifted to rest his back against the door and faced Coley with his left arm resting along the back of the seat. "Nobody expected you to get involved in an orgy with a whore and a street fight. We had to improvise."

Coley took a deep breath and let it out slowly.

"Yeah," he said. "I'm sorry about all that. And I'm very embarrassed. I ought to have been in charge and I wasn't."

"It's behind us, now," the man said. "It doesn't do any good to look back. We have much ahead to worry about. There's a fork in the road when you get over this hill. Keep to the left."

…

For an hour or more we passed through groves of cactus and trees I'd never seen before. On the passenger side of the car the sun was setting behind the low mountains, leaving a deep ochre glow. Coley turned on the headlights but it was still too early for them to make a difference.

The thickening darkness turned the tall cactuses into half-human figures that crowded closer and closer to the road. A sudden pool of shadow became for a moment a boulder in the road, or an enormous hole. I sank down into the seat, trying not to think.

Monk said he had to piss so we pulled over and stopped for a while. When I got out and took a couple of steps the blood came back into my legs. The Mexican picked up a handful of pebbles and flung them in an arc like he was sowing seeds.

Quickly back in the car again, I was waiting for the sound of the engine and the motion of the road to put me to sleep when I saw Coley's hand adjusting the rearview mirror.

"There's a car behind us," he said.

"Slow down." The Mexican's voice was dry.

"I'd rather know why." Coley shifted in his seat and sat taller.

"Do as I tell you."

Monk was snoring.

Coley let the car overtake us and pull into our path. He looked uneasily at the Mexican.

"Stay close," the man said.

We followed the car, an old black Cadillac that had been opulent when new but was now rusted and worn, obscene as a painted old whore. It pulled off the road and parked behind a ridge of boulders, and we pulled off and parked behind it. We sat there in the silent semidarkness and waited for whatever was going to happen. The Mexican scratched the back of his head and seemed to relax into the seat. Monk was still snoring—deep, rattly breaths that would stop so long that he might have been dead and then start again with a jerk and snort. Coley was staring at the Cadillac. I was staring at Coley. We sat that way for a long time. Then a slender girl of nineteen or so stepped out of the car into our headlights. When she turned toward us, I thought she looked pretty.

The Mexican reached over and cut the lights, then the driver of the Cadillac did the same. The girl came up to the Mexican's window. They spoke in Spanish, then she went back to the other car. I heard a car door open and close, then another. I squinted to see. Monk stirred beside me and grunted.

When the girl came back to our car again she was swinging a backpack in one hand. Behind her strolled the skinny kid from the jail. Not a kid exactly: he was about my age but he had a face as soft as a boy's, innocent-looking, like it would be easy to break it. He had a backpack, too.

"OK, then," said Coley.

"What? . . . What?" Monk snorted, sitting up.

Without speaking, the young woman opened the door and climbed over Monk and wedged in beside me. The skinny kid got in front, and the tall, gray-haired man scooted over.

"Greetings, amigos," the skinny kid said, in a voice much deeper than I would have expected it to be. The woman's hair was blowing across my face. Monk was sitting forward, trying to take everything in.

"Does she speak English?" Coley asked, indicating the woman with a jerk of his head.

"Why should she?" the skinny kid asked.

"No reason."

"She is a good soldier. She is my sister."

The talk went on, but it was muffled. Beside me, the girl had taken off her blouse, and she was tugging her legs out of her pants. She wadded the clothes and placed them in my lap like they belonged there. I tried to be as casual as she was as she pulled a suit of tightly rolled combat fatigues out of her backpack. Monk sat back to make room, his eyes glued to the road. I know he was aching to see her in her bra with her pants off, but he was too shy to look. He turned his head away and looked out the side window. I glanced at her and shifted over to give her more room. Then I looked again. I wanted to squeeze my legs together but I was afraid I would come if I did.

The camouflage outfit she put on looked pretty corny to me.

. . .

Monk and the girl were asleep. The backpack and the girl's clothes were on the floor at her feet. In the front seat the older Mexican was lighting a cigarette. His match went out and the skinny kid flicked a lighter. The older guy dragged on the cigarette and groaned and settled back into the seat. The cigarette jerked when he talked.

"You come for what, gringo? Adventure, no?"

"No," Coley said. "Even gringos can believe in something."

"What do you know of what we are doing?"

"What I don't know, I can learn."

"You are willing to learn?"

"That's what I said."

"Then listen."

"I'm listening."

"I will tell you a story."

I'm going to tell you a story, my father said every Friday evening after supper, and then he would take from the bookcase in the living room a thick blue volume with the title *Worthwhile Stories for Every Day* printed on the spine in bright gold. There was a story about Dirty Tom, who came to regret never washing his face; there was one about Little Late Molly, who had to answer in hard ways for never getting anywhere on time; Untruthful Tess came to grief for the lies she told; Selfish Oscar doomed himself to misery for not thinking about others; Lazy Ned learned the cost of indulgence. There were more ways to come to grief in that book than there were in the Bible.

The skinny one lit a cigarette and looked out the window at nothing. Marta—but you don't know her name yet—stirred beside me.

"Fifteen years ago," the old man went on, "this boy was thirteen; the girl was not yet five . . ."

Monk was grunting in his sleep and beginning to snore. The woman's head slid onto his big, round shoulder. The snoring stopped and everything was quiet except for the old man's voice and the sound of the car.

"Their father was editor of a small newspaper. He was arrested because of handbills that were printed on his presses. It was not their father who had printed the handbills. It was the brother of their father. It was I, I must tell you, and a hundred others, lawyers, plumbers, teachers. Sometimes we have killed an officer in the secret police, when we could. With poison, gun, car, knife, whatever. A woman who saw me swore she saw my brother. I was in the hills and knew nothing of this until much later. He was arrested, of course.

In a room under the earth they interrogated him for three days. He told them nothing because he knew nothing.

"But that is not true. He could have told them it was I. He could have told them that. But he told them nothing. The irony—there must always be an irony—is this: for all the years that I had been involved, from the time I stood with him at his wedding with a gun in my coat, he tried to dissuade me from what I was doing. He believed, or I will say he wanted to believe, that things are what they are and that we are born to live life as we find it.

" 'Things will work out,' he would say, 'things are not so bad.'

" 'I have a good job, now' he would say. 'I have children, a beautiful wife, a good wife. You must see how everything is exaggerated.'

"So they arrested him and took him for questioning. How confused he must have been, frightened and confused. Still for two days he said nothing. Then they brought him his wife.

"They strapped him to a wooden chair and brought her before him. He cried to them, begged them. She stood without moving in the middle of the room. What they had already done to her no one can say, but at this moment she stood with her clothes in perfect order and her hair pressed into shape and stared at her husband.

"The Colonel, the examiner, in his green uniform and his high boots, touched his finger to his cap for the lady and left the room. Only the guards were left. And my brother and his wife.

"One of the guards, the person from whom I learned this, was one of us. His fortune was to stand silently and witness the torture so that he could tell us what the police had learned. Remember the name of Hernando Toledo. He is the greatest hero of the revolution. He saved many lives. At one time he was ordered to drive splints under the thumbnails of a young boy. He did that. He jammed the first splint in quickly so that the boy fainted. Two years after the incident of my brother, he joined with four other guards in the rape of a young woman. On the order of the Colonel he choked her to death. He threw her head into her husband's cell.

"The next day, when the Colonel walked into the place for questioning, two floors under the ground where rats ran from the screams of the prisoners, we lost Hernando Toledo. The Colonel had with him a child, a girl perhaps of six years. He was holding her hand and he was smiling. He looked at the guards and swung the child up in his arms as a father might do and took off her dress. He said for one of the guards to bring in the child's father. Hernando Toledo took his pistol from his holster and shot the little girl in the back of the head. The bullet went out her forehead and into the neck of the Colonel. He dropped the child and fell into the blood of both.

"Hernando Toledo then turned the pistol on the other three guards and killed them where they stood. No one responded to the shots because it was not uncommon for the sound of a pistol to come from that room. Hernando Toledo simply walked out the door and up the stairs and into the night.

"He arrived in the first hours of the morning at my house. He told me what had come to pass. I went to get him a drink. When I returned he was dead. He had wrapped his coat around the pistol so that the shot would not bring the police."

Ten miles I guess went by before Coley said anything.

"I couldn't have stood it, either."

"You cannot compare yourself to that man. What have you done? What do you know? You know nothing."

The old man's voice was calm.

"It was not that he could not stand it. Not that he could not watch it. Not that he could not. There is nothing a person despises that he cannot abide if he must. Hernando Toledo had to destroy his body because his soul was lost already. He had been three years with the Colonel. We should have sent another in his place but there was no other. And then he knew it was too late. When he pushed into that young woman and took her breasts like fruit, when he did what he did with the other guards holding her down, there was suddenly a joy in it. He fell on her when he was through and whispered for her to love him, to forgive him. She screamed and continued screaming until the Colonel ordered him to kill her. He thought of her every day and knew in his horror that he wanted to have another such woman, to have something like that to happen again. One takes on the smell of the devil.

"When he saw the dress of the little girl fall to the floor he was aroused. He told me these things and then he killed himself.

"Before the sun rose we buried him in my yard where six others lie with dirt on their eyes and no stone to remember them. All of them are heroes. But all of them together, all of us living, are not worth so much as Hernando Toledo.

"Others have given their lives, some their children. He gave his soul."

The skinny man lit a cigarette. The girl stirred. Coley sat as if he were in the car by himself, looking at the road. The old man took the cigarette from the skinny man, who didn't object but didn't light another.

"My brother's wife was brought in.

"'Tell them,' she said.

"He said nothing.

"'You must tell them something.'

"'I must not,' he said.

"The Colonel came into the room then, smiling as he always smiled. Riding in his arms was a figure not four feet tall with yellow skin and eyes so small they were almost not there at all, peepholes under a bull's brow. The head was bald and brilliant in the garish light. His stubby arms were tight about the Colonel's neck and his head jerked from one position to another as he wrinkled his face like a near-sighted man. He tried to struggle out of the Colonel's arms, grunting and beating the air with his short arms. The Colonel handed him to one of the stronger guards and walked over to stand by my brother's wife.

"'I will enjoy watching this,' he said. 'I hope you will not give us the information we seek too quickly.'

"There was a short squeal and the dwarf leapt from the guard's arms to land on the back of the woman. She fell onto the floor, struggling but making no sound. The guards rushed to hold her while the dwarf tore off all her clothes. Each took a hand or a foot and they spread her out.

"My brother started to speak. The Colonel struck him in the mouth with his gloved hand.

"The Colonel ordered her to her feet. He took off his boots and forced her to put them on. He ordered her to march back and forth across the room. He took off his colonel's hat and placed it on her head.

"'Ha!' he cried. 'Ha! Ha!'

"He told her to march again.

"A guard beat a tattoo on the wall with his club. The Colonel clapped his hands.

"'Stop!' my brother cried. 'Stop! I will tell you!'

"The guards looked at the Colonel.

"'Continue,' he said, and hit my brother again across the mouth.

"They used her for half an hour, stopping for fondling when they chose to.

"'Now!' the Colonel cried.

"The guards pulled her to the floor and spread her for the dwarf. The Colonel leaned against the wall. My brother was screaming like a madman and pulling at his bonds.

"When the dwarf had emptied himself he crawled up her body and took her throat in his hands. He turned in that position and looked at the Colonel. The Colonel nodded and the fingers closed around the throat of my brother's wife. Her face became red and then white and her body jerked two times exactly and she was still.

"My brother stopped screaming.

"'Well,' the Colonel said. 'You think now the bitch is dead you have no reason to talk. Many have felt this way.'

"My brother said nothing.

"They brought his children into the room. Marta cried when she saw her mother. Flavio was stunned for a moment and then he tore loose from his guard and lunged at the shape sitting upon his black-booted mother. The dwarf threw him against a far wall so hard it broke an arm. Marta stopped crying.

" 'I will tell you what I know,' my brother said.

"The Colonel ordered my brother's hands unbound and called for paper. As one of the guards placed the paper and a pen on the arm of my brother's chair he turned so that his pistol was nearly in my brother's grasp. The gun was out of the holster as the guard shouted a warning and dropped to the floor. My brother pulled the trigger once but there was only a click. By then one of the guards had drawn his own pistol and shot Flavio's father through the heart.

"The Colonel was in a rage. He ordered a beating for the careless guard who was of course, as you know, Hernando Toledo. He was sentenced also to another year in the dungeon.

" 'The children must be disposed of,' the Colonel complained.

" 'I will do it,' Toledo told him. 'It is the least I can do to atone for my carelessness.'

"Hernando Toledo took them to my home. I was, as I have told you, out of the city, but there were many staying under that roof. Flavio and Marta found new parents there and a cause that would sustain them.

"How do I know," he asked Coley abruptly, "that you are not the CIA?"

"Come on," Coley answered, letting his shoulders drop. "You have to know better than that."

The old man slid down in the seat then and seemed to fall asleep. Flavio awoke and looked out the window. We came to a country store set close to the road, with an electric light over the door and an old, bubble-headed, hand-cranked gasoline pump in front.

I leaned back and closed my eyes.

. . .

When I woke up the car was stopped. I thought I was alone until I heard a stirring in the front seat. I raised up and saw Coley lying on his back with his arms folded on his chest and his legs hanging out the open door on the driver's side. It was just getting light but I was already sweating. We were parked in the foothills, probably of the mountains we had been driving toward all night, just off the road under an overhanging bluff. I got out of the car. A little ways away the others were sitting around a small fire. I walked over to join them. The smell of beans made me hungry.

"Is there enough to go around?"

"There better be," Monk grunted. He was sitting on his haunches watching the pot.

Marta took the beans off the fire, portioned them onto four flat rocks, and gave Monk and me each a spoon. The old man and Flavio took from their clothes knives with long, flat blades. I knew that I was being patronized, but it was all right. Monk was holding the rock up to his chin and pushing the beans into his mouth.

Marta speared a piece of meat with her knife. She spoke in Spanish to Flavio. His eyes followed her to the car. I thought of what Flavio and Marta might have been doing those Sunday afternoons we sat on Mount Carmel, drinking beer and talking about philosophy and girls and listening to Patsy Cline while I hobbled around on an ingrown toenail.

...

What marvelous hills these would have been to run through when we were ten, pointing our pistols and saying *Bang!* and clutching our chests and spinning around to collapse joint by joint until we lay on the earth like grass, shot dead.

It was great fun to die, more fun to die than to kill someone.

...

"We part now," the old man said. "We will soon leave Mexico. Flavio and Marta must not go farther together. It is important that one of them get through. She will go to the east, and you will go with her. A boat is waiting for you. I will go with Flavio. We will arrive at the same place if luck is with us."

"How much farther?" Monk asked him.

"It is close."

"I don't know why you're troubling yourselves with us," Coley said.

"I am not sure, either," the man answered.

"What good are we to you?"

"Who can say?"

The man shrugged, and he took his knife and drew a map in the dirt.

"If all goes well, we will meet in three days. It will not be easy."

"It won't be any worse than the Grand Canyon," Monk said. "I went down the side of that thing on a mule."

The old man and Flavio gathered up their things while Marta buried the fire. Then the old man started handing out guns from the car. He gave Flavio and Marta heavy-looking army rifles. They loaded the guns and strapped belts of ammo around their waists. He gave Coley a bolt-action hunting rifle and a box of shells. He gave Monk a pistol—I learned later that it was the .38 Coley had brought—and he gave me an old long-barreled revolver that must have weighed ten pounds. Monk and I fingered the guns, trying to look natural with them. The little pistol looked lost in his fist, and it was all I could do to hold my revolver out in front of me. We traded without speaking. Marta gave Monk and me some bullets and we loaded the guns. The old man carried a Luger that looked like it came through World War II.

"What about the car?" Coley asked. "It's not going to be here when we get back."

"If you get back," the old man said, "it will not matter much. If you do not get back, it will not matter at all."

"Right," Coley said, like a soldier.

"Hey, man," Monk said. "I got a new pair of shoes in my suitcase. I got all kinds of things in there."

Flavio slapped him on the shoulder.

"I will see you in San Felipe in two days," Flavio said. Then to Marta, "Nos vemos. Ten cuidado." He took her in his arms and kissed her, then he and the old man were gone.

"We don't have any water," Monk said.

"I guess Marta knows that," Coley answered.

"I hope so."

"Don't worry about it." He fixed his grip on the rifle.

Monk looked back at the car.

"I sure hate to go off and leave all that stuff. Paul's going to really be mad about the car."

"You can drive it back if you want to," Coley told him. "You don't have to go with us."

"There's not enough gas and I don't know where I am."

"Some days it's like that," Coley said.

"Just can it!" Monk said. "What's happened is, I've been kidnapped! You start out just running around, you don't think about where you're going, and all of a sudden you're knee deep in it. This ain't where I meant to be. It ain't even close."

"It's where you are," Coley said.

"Don't be philosophical," Monk growled. "I can't stand it when you get philosophical."

I liked Coley a lot, but I knew what Monk meant.

…

Since we didn't know what else to do, we followed Marta up the gradually rising ground. These were not like the hills at home where everything is farther away than it looks. These hills were closer than they seemed to be, and high suddenly, and hard, with sharp edges.

Coley stumbled and caught himself, sending loose rocks down the slope. He picked up his pace to overtake Marta, who was up ahead of us.

A bullet hit the rocks not three feet from my leg and then I heard a gunshot.

"Get down!" Coley shouted, but we were already on our faces. I needed to go to the bathroom.

…

I could smell the earth, inches from my face. I could feel it against my hands. I could feel the earth pushing back against my belly each time I took a breath. I had an erection and didn't know why.

A rock burrowed into my side. Monk was breathing like a bull. I suddenly felt very cold. I thought about getting hit by a bullet, how it would feel. I thought about dying.

Kle-check! That's as close as I can get to the sound of it. Marta made a motion for us to follow her, so we did, crawling on our elbows the length of a city block. I could feel my chin tightening. I thought of my mother. I could smell her lap, the way it smelled when I went to sleep in church with my head buried in the dotted swiss of her Sunday dress.

Follow the gleam, they sang. She would stay seated when they stood because I was lying there with my head in her lap.

Stand up, stand up for Jesus, Ye soldiers of the Cross, Onward, Christian Soldiers, Lead, Kindly Light.

Kle-check! Kle-check!

Marta led us toward a shallow cave, not much more than a yawn in the mountainside.

Kle-check!

"Who is it up there?" Coley whispered. "Why are they shooting at us?"

"Not shooting at *us,*" she said. "At *me.*"

Kle-check!

Monk slid ten or twelve feet down the mountain, digging his fingers into the pebbly dirt, grunting and complaining. He stopped with his foot against the tip of a rock.

Marta shouted to him in Spanish. Coley said it in English.

"Be still, Monk. Don't move."

He was spread-eagled on the slope, his big body as tight against the hill as he could press it.

Marta spoke to Coley in Spanish. Coley translated.

"Keep down as flat as you can. Crawl up like a snake."

Monk came grunting toward us, wiggling inch by inch like a giant lizard. They were still shooting at us.

When Monk was finally panting beside us again we continued to climb until we reached the shallow cave. Marta disappeared into it, then we were all inside and the shooting stopped. There was more than enough room for the four of us.

"Who are they?" Coley asked.

"The others," she answered in English.

We sat for a long time. I was getting thirsty. I turned to the back of the cave and pissed into the darkness.

"Let's get out of here," Monk demanded.

"Let him go," Marta said to Coley.

Kop-chingg.

It hit inside the cave. Marta took her rifle and crouched near the entrance. I held my little pistol and knelt beside her. Coley took a position on the other side of the opening, on the edge of the sunlight.

"Take the safety off," he said.

I flipped it so the red dot showed. I was mad at myself that he had to remind me but I loved him for it.

Monk squatted by Coley. He held the revolver with both hands.

Marta raised her rifle, took aim, and squeezed the trigger. It made a terrible sound in our little grave. Whoever was out there shot back. I crawled forward and tried to look out but Marta pressed her hand on top of my head and pushed me down.

I saw something red flash maybe a hundred feet down the slope. I saw it again. It was a red sleeve, worn by someone who meant to kill me. He didn't know who I was. He didn't know anything about me. He didn't have any right to kill me. I lay down and braced my elbow on the ground and fired. The sleeve stayed where it was. I thought I would just shoot him in the arm. I thought I could do that. But I shot again and still the sleeve stayed where it was.

Then Marta shot again. We heard a cry, a sort of curse, but it might have been someone calling out orders.

I couldn't see the red sleeve anymore.

Marta yelled something at Coley and ran out into the sunlight, bent low, firing as she ran with the rifle held at her side. I took her place at the mouth of the cave and imagined that I gave her some sort of cover with what now seemed to be a popgun in my hand. Bang, bang. Marta fell. From behind the rock a man in a red shirt scurried away up the mountainside. His right arm seemed to be hanging loose at his side.

Coley shot at him. I didn't think he would do that when the man was running away. Anyway, he missed him.

I saw Marta fire from the ground where she was lying and the man fell forward without raising a hand to break his fall. He rolled ten or fifteen feet down the mountain toward us.

Coley slapped me on the shoulder as he ran out to check on Marta. I waited for more shots but there weren't any. I looked around for Monk and saw him, a shadow of him, at the back of the cave.

I ran to join Coley and Marta and found them standing over the red shirt. Not far away there was another body. Coley put his rifle down. Marta let herself fall back against a large rock, breathing heavily. Then I saw that one of the bodies was not dead.

The red shirt rolled over and the head sticking out of it opened its eyes and its mouth, then the eyes looked past us, past the clouds, past everything, then the clouds settled into the eyes and the head lay still.

I climbed back to the cave alone. I wanted to vomit, but I managed to hold it back. I considered that those people had tried to kill me—people with names and families and underwear—they had tried to kill me. I found Monk sitting down, pressed against a side of the cave, half-hidden between the ridges that ran down the walls like the ribs of a whale.

"What's the matter, Monk?"

"I'm hit. Where's Coley?"

"Where? Let me see?"

He pulled away.

"Where's Coley?"

"I'm right here, Monk."

I turned in a wave of relief that almost took the bones out of my legs. Coley and Marta were silhouetted in the blazing entrance, walking slowly toward us. When they had leaned their guns against the wall of the cave, Monk got to his feet and waved his revolver.

"Back off," he yelled.

Coley and Marta looked at each other. Monk swung the revolver at me and I put my pistol down at my feet.

"Get out of here!" he said. "Get away from the guns."

We all moved toward the light and stepped out into it. Monk followed us and stood in the cave entrance, nearly blocking it.

"Monk," Coley said. "What are you doing?"

"He told me he was hit," I said.

"Shut up," Monk barked at me. Then he swung the gun back toward Coley.

"Give me the keys."

"What keys?"

"The keys. Don't mess with me."

Coley reached into his pocket and brought them out.

"It's a long drive, Monk. It's a long way back to the car and it's a long way home."

"Not as long as where she's going," he said. "Just give them to me."

Coley tossed them. When Monk grabbed them out of the air he stood there for a moment like he was surprised that he had them. He looked at us like it was all just a joke, then ran off down the mountainside. He stopped once and looked back at us, laid the revolver down on the ground, and ran on, stumbling and pulling himself up again, his shadow sliding over the rocks ahead of him.

When he was almost out of sight we heard a shot and he fell. We couldn't be sure if the shot had taken him down or if he'd slipped again. Later I thought I saw him crest a rise farther on, still running, but I wasn't sure. It might've been the shadow of a cloud.

Coley started to go check on him but Marta blocked his way.

"He might be in trouble."

"No," she said. She recovered the revolver and handed it to Coley. He stuck it in his belt.

"Marta," he said. "I've got to go see."

"No," she said again. "He is gone."

We got to the top of that mountain—not much of a mountain, really—and down the other side before we stopped to rest. We found water in the little valley and ate some bread that Marta had. Then it was dark and we couldn't see to go on.

...

I never learned to know Coley the way I wanted to, except in flashes. I had come with him to a foreign country where I couldn't speak the language and was afraid to go on and couldn't go back. Now I was looking at him, asleep with his ankles crossed and his hands locked over that strange, impatient heart. I still didn't know who he was. Or who I was, either. I was pretty sure that at least one of us was crazy.

I know I fell asleep finally because I woke up from a dream. I dreamed I was Siamese twins and one side of me spoke Spanish. I was pushing Monk up a mountain but every time I got him to the top he turned into a dwarf and started chasing Marta, who was naked.

I woke up cold. Marta was sleeping on her stomach and her right arm was thrown over Coley's chest. I got up and pissed and tried to go back to sleep but I couldn't curl my body up tight enough to get warm. Anyway it was getting light. I got up and walked around for a while and kicked at stones. Then I could hear Marta and Coley talking. I didn't know what they were saying but they sounded like they were telling secrets. I waited until they began to move around and then I joined them, yawning.

For breakfast we had water and bread. Coley and I had grown scratchy beards. He had a rifle over his shoulder. We both had guns in our belts. We had been shot at and we had been hungry. I thought I was a soldier of fortune. I thought Coley was a soldier.

Overnight he had changed. He walked like he knew where he was going, walking beside Marta, saying something in Spanish now and then, shifting the weight of his rifle. His hair was blown by the wind that cut around the rocks. Sweat brightened his face. If he had known the way he might have broken into a run.

My life before seemed like a flat backdrop for the stage where all of this was happening. The home I grew up in, the upstairs bedroom where I read books and masturbated and slept, the Roxy theater. Salina Mae Becker and Lettie Tuttle and Rosalie Powers and the others, all of that now seemed part of a single, simple day. There were only two times, before now and now; only two places, not here and here.

We were getting closer to the ocean. We could smell it long before we came in sight of the settlement at the edge of the bay, where a boat would be waiting for us. A long time ago it was too late to turn back.

...

There were dogs in the village. We could hear them barking at each other as we sat waiting for night, looking down on the narrow streets and the flat square clay houses between us and the ocean. For a while there were lights, people talking, visiting in the streets. Women stood in front of their houses, men went in and out of cantinas or stood in the streets singing or arguing their way home, and then until most of the lights went out there was the shouting of children. Over it all was the barking of dogs. From our side of the village, a hoarse challenge; from the other, an answer.

Here and there a light still burned, maybe where somebody was sick or there was a game of cards. Along the bay some of the boats had lights. Marta pointed toward one of them.

"Eso es."

"How can you tell from here?" Coley asked in English, but she had already started down the hill.

The bottoms of my feet hurt. I was beginning to walk on the sides of them, like my shoes were run over. There were some kids in grade school that always had shoes run over like that. A girl came to school once in an older pair of boy's shoes and I saw that they were mine. My mother had given them to the Missionary Society rummage sale.

I slid down from a horse when I was about eight and hit on my heels. The electricity shot all the way to my shoulders and out to my elbows. I felt that now, every time I took a step. I tried to walk on the balls of my feet but it didn't help.

I could smell the village before we got to it. At first I thought of chickens. It smelled like a room that's been closed for a long time. The way hair smells when it hasn't been washed. Dirt under country houses. People living too close together. The breath of dogs.

We were walking between the houses. The moon was rising. It caught the metal of the gun barrels and turned Marta's hair to liquid. Dogs sniffed at us and barked. We stepped over a man asleep in the street. We heard a guitar and a woman laughing. Then a huge, growling dog came toward us out of the shadows. Its head was down, with the lips rolled back so that the teeth glistened.

I moved close to Coley.

"No!" Coley said, showing the dog his flat palms. "No!"

The growling stopped.

"No!" Coley patted his hands on the air. I put a hand on my pistol. Coley let the dog sniff the back of his hand, then he was kneeling down, patting the smelly monster.

"Someday you're going to try that," I said, "and you're going to get torn up."

"Maybe," he allowed.

We slipped quickly between the mud houses, the wooden shutters, the lopsided carts propped against the walls, the straight chairs waiting outside closed doors, down unrutted roads that may never have seen a car. Once a door opened. A boy of about twelve stopped when he saw me. We looked directly into each other's eyes and he closed the door without a sound.

Beyond the village the land fell away to a narrow beach. Seven or eight small cabin boats, their lights all out now, bumped on the black waves that flashed in the moonlight.

I fell over a bag that righted itself to become in the dim light an old woman all in black, head to toe. She was sitting on a block of wood, leaning against the side of a hovel only a few yards from the sea. She looked up at us and opened her mouth. Her eyes rolled around and then her head rolled around. With what seemed a terrible effort she got to her feet, crossed herself, said "Diablos," and hobbled away into the darkness. Coley and Marta had gone on, toward the boats. I hurried to join them.

The main differences in the boats, so far as I could see at first, were the names: *Juanita, Santa Maria,* that sort of thing. Then I saw that one of them was a good deal larger than the others, wider and longer and lower in the water. It was *La Vida.* "Life." Fishing nets and rope hung everywhere, but I guessed it wasn't a fishing boat.

We climbed aboard up a sort of stepladder that hung over the side. When we moved together across the deck it rose behind us and fell beneath us.

Marta disappeared into an unlit cabin and we followed her, stooping through the hatch and feeling our way down the ladder. I heard the sound of curtains being drawn and the click of a lighter. The lighter clicked again. Marta cursed and someone laughed. A match was lit and touched to the wick of a kerosene lamp that hung from the ceiling, and a yellow light filled the little cabin.

Five shapes materialized around me, Coley and Marta and three others: a blonde man in khaki pants and a short-sleeved Hawaiian shirt, an enormous woman a head and a half taller than the man, and—on a bunk to our right—what I took to be a child, a boy.

The blonde man was chewing on a dead pipe. He grinned around it and studied us, sucking on it unpleasantly. He nodded as if we were being introduced. The woman may have weighed three hundred pounds. She wore the biggest overalls I'd ever seen and a bleached-out work shirt. Snuff swelled the flesh under her lower lip. Her mouth worked slowly and she stared at us out of small eyes that were almost buried in her face. Her hair in the lamplight seemed almost orange. She might have been thirty or sixty. She nodded and spat into a coffee can she held in her hand.

The figure on the bunk let out a long sigh and got to his feet. He was a short, wiry man, maybe four and a half feet tall, maybe less. He had on walking shorts and an undershirt and the old-style high-top canvas tennis shoes with knee socks. White hair curled over his ears. He took Marta's rifle and Coley's and dropped them onto the cot where he'd been lying. I started to hand him my pistol but he didn't want it.

"This here is Pete," he said, laying a hand on the air in the general direction of the giant woman. "She's my wife. Common law. She's the captain of this ship. She's got three bullets lost in her somewhere." The orange head nodded. An enormous arm came up and wiped brown trickles from her chin. She said something in Spanish and Marta answered. The little man slapped the blonde man in the belly with the back of his hand.

"This here is Mr. Douglas. He's come here as a magazine writer. He ain't one of us. We're mostly romantic by nature and you might say by occupation. He represents the more or less classical view of things. Your basic cynic. Got a lot of snappin' turtle in him. When he gets hold of you he don't let go till it thunders."

Mr. Douglas took the pipe out of his mouth, hit it a couple of times against his thigh, and sat down on the bunk, shoving the guns back. He crossed his legs and put the dead pipe back in his mouth. No one moved to shake hands with anyone.

"Sit," the little man said. "We got to wait for the others."

"What others?" Coley asked, uneasily.

"Flavio's number one man. And his woman, of course."

"Of course," Coley said.

Coley nudged Marta toward the other bunk and they both sat. I sat opposite them, beside the reporter. Marta and Pete began to talk in Spanish. I got the feeling that the little man didn't speak Spanish and that his wife didn't speak English.

Pete left us after a while and went up on deck. The little man followed her, then came back down the stairs.

"I'm John Quincy Adams," he said.

"I'm pleased to meet you, Mr. Adams," Coley said.

"Mr. President," he said.

"Mr. President," Coley said. "I'm . . ." but the President raised a hand and cut him off.

"I don't want to know your names," he said. He turned and went up the steps. Coley and Marta and I looked at each other until Marta lay down on one of the cots and stretched out.

"Ah," she said, "Ah," and she closed her eyes. Coley sat down on the floor beside her. He rested his head on the edge of her cot with an arm across her legs. I started to follow the President up the ladder.

"I wouldn't go up there," Coley warned.

I backed down and sat on the vacant cot. I could feel the boat rocking.

I lay down on the cot and closed my eyes.

I woke up on the high seas about to wet my pants. I was alone. I got up and opened the door opposite the stairs, hoping it was a toilet. It was filled with kegs and boxes. I made it up the ladder as quickly as I could and stepped out into daylight.

The deck was crowded. Captain Pete was standing at the wheel. John Quincy Adams was sitting on the deck with his legs crossed under him, writing in a notebook, trying to keep the leaves from turning in the wind. Coley was looking out over the water. Marta was sitting on the cabin block with her hand underneath her for a cushion, talking to a man and a woman I didn't know. They were dressed the same as she was, fatigues and grease and dirt.

"That's the number one man?" I whispered to Coley.

"Yeah," he said. "He calls the girl Angela. I don't know what his name is, but I don't think he likes us very much."

"How come?"

"You know how come."

"Hey, Yanqui!" This was the man. He was coming toward us, stomping the deck with his boots, grinning through a week's growth of beard. It went with the uniform. I moved away from the railing as he moved toward us.

He put a hand on Coley's shoulder. He was thin and tall.

"You want to fight, no cierto?"

Coley didn't answer him.

"You want blood, no? Sangre, no?"

"Get off my back," Coley snapped without moving.

"Hey, Yanqui," the rebel sang, rocking into Coley's face. "I don't understand so good English. Talk slow."

"You understand," Coley told him and turned away. The man looked at me then and stepped toward me with his elephant boots. He took hold of my arm and I thought he was going to jerk it off. I looked around for help. He put his arms around me and lifted me into the air.

"You come to help us, hey gringo? You save my country. I love you." He swung me around two or three times. My feet swung out over the water. He brought me back in and gave me a couple of squeezes. I nearly passed out. I could hear Coley's voice, then Pete's, and the man dropped me to my feet. My knees folded and I fell on the deck. I was trying not to cry. There was pain in my chest.

When I could focus again I saw him—the rebel—talking to Angela. They seemed to be arguing. Coley and Marta were helping me get up and I realized that my pants were wet.

. . .

The President came down the stairs and looked for a moment at Coley and me. We were sitting opposite each other on the two cots.

"Done!" he shouted. "Done! You want to hear it?"

"Hear what?" I asked him.

"The poem."

"I didn't know you were a poet," Coley said.

The President opened a black notebook and slammed it shut again.

"Well," he demanded.

"Let's hear it," Coley said.

"When I have fears that I may cease to be . . ." he began, and cleared his throat. He looked at each of us for some kind of reaction. I took my cue from Coley's face, which was intent. I looked intent, too. Mr. Adams turned around and climbed back up onto the deck.

. . .

Whatever was had for breakfast, I missed it. Dinner, which was a long time coming, was two sandwiches apiece and a cup of coffee. My stomach was too tight to take it very well. Coley and Marta ate with me in the cabin. I was more scared than I was with the peasants in the road or the soldiers on the mountain. I thought about the rebel with the heavy boots. I imagined my arms being broken. I thought about being choked until the gristle in my throat cracked. I thought about my teeth cracking under the force of his fist. A coward dies a thousand deaths. I thought about swimming for shore. I thought about shooting myself in the leg.

I could hear him walking around on the deck. I could hear Pete laughing and shouting.

I had finished my sandwiches and the last sip of my coffee when Angela came down the ladder. She said something to Marta and they went up together. Coley looked at me a minute, slapped me once on the knee, and went after them. I tried to go back to sleep but I couldn't. I was a stowaway on the Ark, the only creature that didn't belong to a pair. When the flood was over my kind would die out.

...

Coley and I were sitting on the cots drinking coffee while he tried to talk me into going on deck again when the reporter came jauntily—not jauntily, exactly, but like a reporter— down the ladder.

"What are you two doing here?"

"Tending our gardens," Coley said.

The reporter took the pipe out of his mouth. He looked at us like we were children lying about why we weren't in school.

"I know you, friend," he said, flipping the *f* out with his lower lip like it was stuck there. "I know you," he repeated, straining. "I know you from way back. You're everywhere I go. Political missionaries. You're going to get your asses shot off, if you have the guts to stick around that long. You liberals make me sick. You're going to bring your college education down here and make everything all right. You don't know a thing about what's going on down here. You lie to yourself and you lie to everybody else. You make me sick."

"Sorry," Coley said, lifting his eyes over the rim of his coffee cup. "You're here for your reason, I'm here for mine."

"OK," the reporter said. "OK. You're a political missionary, and you're a liar. Mercenaries don't lie. A good homegrown revolutionary doesn't lie. Political missionaries lie all the time. All they do is lie."

"Bull," Coley said, standing up and jamming his hands in his pockets. The boat leaned and dipped and Coley fell back onto his bunk. The reporter shot a hand out and caught the stairs to steady himself.

"You want to save your own soul," the reporter said, "so you find yourself a revolution. You want to wash away the guilt in somebody else's blood."

"What guilt?" Coley answered.

"You know what guilt."

"You really do have a hair up your ass, don't you," Coley kind of sneered. "I thought reporters weren't supposed to take sides."

"I'm not a reporter."

"He said you were."

"He said I was a writer."

"A magazine writer."

"Correct."

"I see."

"No, you don't. You don't see anything at all."

When I first saw the reporter—the writer—he didn't seem old at all. Twenty-five, maybe, or thirty. Now I could see that he was a lot older.

"Let me tell you something," he said slowly. "Take this to heart." He placed the tips of his fingers on his chest and then he shook them at me as if he might be sprinkling me with water. "You're not about to do any good with these people."

He looked back and forth at both of us and snorted and put his hands in his pockets.

"Hmmh! OK. You might help them win the war, if you can call this mess a war, but then what?

"If you're still alive, you'll all sit down to see how the country ought to be run, and you might have a suggestion, and they won't know what you're talking about. You'll all use the same words, like constitution, but you won't mean the same thing when you say it. To them it's just a piece of paper. All they've ever really believed in is the big man. When he goes bad—finally too bad to stand—they get rid of him if they can and get another one. They never catch on. There's no way out of it."

He seemed old as a mummy, swaying from one foot to the other against the rocking of the boat.

Coley spoke from the bunk where he was still seated, the cold coffee cup in his hands again.

"If we didn't prop up every right-wing dictatorship in the hemisphere they wouldn't last a month."

"There were right-wing dictatorships here before the United States existed, my friend. How do you explain that?"

"I'm not a historian," Coley answered.

"What are you?"

They stared at each other.

"You think these are the good guys," the reporter went on, "and that the General and his soldiers are the bad guys. You have a lot to learn about your commandos. Let me tell you something. I've seen scores of bodies they've left with their throats cut open and the tongue pulled out the slit." He pantomimed the act with a slash and jerk of his head. "La corbata, they call it. The necktie. The tongue is considerably longer than it seems to be. It hangs way down when you pull it out that way."

"That's sick," I said.

"You'd better believe it," the reporter snapped. "And I'll tell you what else is sick. It's sick for you missionaries to come trotting down here to kill the dragon when you don't know that the lady in the cave is a retarded bitch the dragon has been taking care of most of her life because she couldn't take care of herself. I've seen it, kid. I've seen them chop down old men and I've seen them kill girls coming out of classrooms. They killed a man and his wife because they let their son be drafted."

"Some of that may be true," Coley admitted.

The reporter smiled.

"We're going to win," Coley said.

"Of course you are," the reporter agreed. "I never doubted you were going to win." He sat down on the cot beside me. "I've known these people since Zapata. Since O'Higgins. Since Bolivar. Listen to me now. Marta's brother, Flavio, it will be his victory. He will win. And what do you think will happen then?"

Coley sat with his elbows on his knees, ready to answer.

"When he is the big man, what will happen? Elections? A free press?"

"Not at first, maybe," Coley started.

"OK, then, a while longer. We will have to wait a while longer. And then a while longer."

"If you feel that way, what are you doing here?"

"I need you," he said.

The rocking of the boat was beginning to make me queasy. Coley rose without saying anything else and went up on deck. I waited for Douglas to turn on me but he didn't. He looked at the lantern swaying against the sway of the boat, making its circle like a dead comet.

The pilot's wheel was jerking and spinning with no one to tend it. The tall rebel and Angela were dancing toward each other and away, together and away, a white handkerchief in her right hand and a red bandana flipping like a whip in his. They stomped on the deck and yelped like dogs. Marta watched, clapping her hands to their rhythm, her face alive with laughter. Coley stood beside her, trying to clap when she did.

Above and behind me I heard the voice of the captain, a soft, mumbled song, very different from the rhythm of the dance. I turned to see her on the roof of the cabin that made a stage in the middle of the deck. The clouds moving behind her made me dizzy. The wind was rising. The boat rocked like a cradle. She was sitting in a large wooden chair on the cabin roof, clumping up and down like the chair was a rocker, holding the President in her arms, singing to him. The pilot's wheel was spinning roulette. Then a plane came out of the blue sky, roaring out of the wind, its wings brilliant and trembling.

Pete sprang to her feet and threw the President into the ocean. She yelled at Angela. There was a scurrying, a splashing, and everyone but Coley and me and the big rebel and the reporter jumped overboard. I ran to the wheel but I didn't know what to do.

"The boat's full of dynamite," Coley told me. "The plane will come back."

It took me a moment to put those two pieces of information together. I was jerking the wheel back and forth.

"Go!" Coley yelled. "Jump!"

The wheel felt good. The boat began to take orders in the rough water: left, right, steady. The boat loved me. I loosened my grip and let it have a little play, then I took control again. I heard the boards underneath me groaning.

Then I saw Coley stumble against the lurching of the deck. Suddenly the hateful rebel with the heavy boots picked Coley up and threw him over the side. He was slinging life jackets in all directions. Then he tore me loose from the wheel and tossed me into the sea. I have always been afraid of water. I grabbed for a jacket as the plane came in again.

Then there was no boat. Only small pieces of wood floating around me. The sea was calm, the air was thin and bright, and I was alone. I was coughing and choking, kicking against the sea. Ten or a hundred yards ahead of me something was bobbing on the surface. I swam toward it until I saw that it was the head of the rebel, the one who had thrown me overboard, floating on a raft of planks. I didn't want to get close but I couldn't stay afloat much longer without resting. I swam toward the raft, hoping the head would roll off before I reached it.

Then I saw that it was not just his head, but all of him. An arm was slung over the boards and the head rested upon it. He was dead. His eyes and his mouth were open and his tongue was hanging out. His teeth were dark with blood. The waves from my flailing arms splashed over the little raft. I could see as I swam closer that his sleeve was caught on a nail. I tore it loose and watched his head and arm slide off and then he was gone.

...

It was a bigger raft than I thought, maybe two feet wide and a yard long. It had come from the bow of the boat—it carried the square white letters of the boat's name, VIDA. I pulled myself onto it until I could relax a little, lying on it longways, and looked around for some sign of land. The squat white letters shimmered just under the surface of the water, a bright, transparent veneer: ES SUEÑO . . . is a dream . . .

...

When I was seven I went to Memphis for the first time. My mother took me to Kress's and I bought an army tent for my toy soldiers. It was real cloth and had a flag on top.

Let the words of my mouth and the meditations of my heart be acceptable unto thy sight O Lord my strength and my redeemer.

I remembered a photograph of my little cousin and me when I was five on the steps of my grandparent's house. My hair was white as cotton. The shadow of my mother, who was taking the picture, could be seen stretching across the grass to the bottom of the steps.

The Lord bless you and keep you, the Lord be merciful unto you, the Lord lift up his countenance upon you and give you peace.

Where the deer and the antelope play.

Ain't I the lucky one?

Amen.

The sun warmed the boards under the layer of water that washed over them. The sun burned into my brain and salt caked on my face and in my hair. My fingers were locked in rigor mortis over the split edges of the raft, dead to the splinters. My feet were still in the water. My wet clothes were like lead.

I vomited into the ocean.

I had no way of keeping track of how much time was passing.

I tried to kick my feet to paddle the raft, but they wouldn't move.

I sent the message again to kick. Nothing happened for a moment and then my right leg moved. The pain was sharp and long and I lay a good while before I tried again. Eventually I had both legs moving a little. There were still needles shooting through, but I managed to create a kind of paddlewheel.

I tried to clear my vision but the brightness and the shimmering of the air and the swelling of my eyes made it impossible.

Something moved off to my right. I thought of sharks, that they had smelled the vomit. I wanted to stop kicking so I wouldn't attract their attention and I wanted to kick harder to escape them. I was trying to get used to the idea of dying.

...

As I pulled away from one of the sharks it waved its arms and shouted at me in Spanish. I stopped kicking as Angela, using an unfastened life jacket, splashed her way toward me. She sort of smiled, catching her breath, and said something I didn't understand. I motioned toward what looked like land ahead of us. We began paddling like two sternwheelers, grunting and spitting water.

Gradually the gray texture we swam toward became solid, and after an hour or so we put our feet down. Our legs were so tired that we used our floats for water crutches and pushed ourselves toward the beach until we could roll off onto the sand. The air around me turned red and then green. I tumbled forward as it turned quickly to black.

...

The sun was still high when I opened my eyes. Angela lay on her belly with her arms out wide. I could see her breathing. Her hair was spread like a shawl. Her fatigues were already drying and her boots were gone. I realized that I should have taken off my shoes when I found myself in the water but I was glad now that I hadn't.

Watching her deep breathing, I felt the start of a hard-on until I considered the difference between sleep and unconsciousness. I was sitting up when I saw Pete coming out of the ocean, waist deep, then knee deep, walking with a heavy, hill-climbing motion. The

President was held in her arms like a rag doll, his head and arms and legs dangling loose, dripping water. She was staring past us, her chin clean of snuff. Her little eyes were red as a rabbit's, translucent and empty. When I thought she would step across me she turned without a word and plodded down the beach, sat down, and drew the President's head to her bosom.

Angela whined and coughed and rolled over onto her back. Through the open front of her fatigues a pale blue ribbon laced along the top of her bra. Sand was glued to the glossy white cloth and the cinnamon skin that rose and fell about it. Sand was on her face and in her hair. I flipped my fingers through my hair to shake the sand out and brushed it from my clothes.

Angela sat up and looked at me like she was accustomed to waking up and seeing me there. She said something I barely heard and didn't understand but I didn't think she was talking to me anyway.

She kept hugging her knees. A few yards away the captain sat in the sand with her feet in shallow water, with John Quincy Adams in her arms, and looked up at the sky. Nothing moved but the water.

I didn't know where Coley was. I didn't know where we were, either, if there were people around or if we were on an island or the mainland. I started toward a wall of thick foliage a good ways from the shore to see if there was a path, any sign of human habitation. There wasn't. I headed south along the shore. There was sand and sea to the right and jungle to the left. Sunset spread like oil on the water, breaking into fire on the small waves. The sun was half into the sea when I got back to Angela and the captain.

She had laid the President down and was going through his pockets, emptying them one by one into her own. When this was done she picked him up in her arms and carried him out into the tide as far as she could walk. Then she began to swim, pulling him by the hair. She went so far we couldn't see her in the fading light. She swam back alone.

She knelt on the sand and I thought she was going to pray. I knelt beside her and Angela stood looking out at the sea. Pete began to build and shape a pile of wet sand. She was sculpting an enormous prick.

At its monumental base she incised in the smooth sand the letters

JQA

RIP

then she stood up and took from each of her front pockets a snuff can, one of Garrett's, and one with no label. She opened the Garrett's, pulled her lower lip away from her teeth, and poured a little snuff into the trough. She grinned at me and the snuff began to show at the corners of her mouth. I looked at Angela. She was breathing like she had been running, her arms loose at her sides. I thought about the pale blue ribbon hiding beneath her coveralls. Suddenly, even more than I wanted to go home and live a long time, I wanted to go lie down with her in the sand. At the time, I didn't have a thought for the dead rebel.

Pete tossed the other snuff can to me. I heard the rattle and pulled off the lid to find a dozen kitchen matches broken to fit, with the bottom half saved for kindling. She began gathering firewood. I put the tin in my pocket and hurried to help her. By dark we had a good blaze going. I went to sleep listening to the women talking softly in Spanish.

By the time the morning sun cleared the mountain I was at least a mile from the campsite, where the sand gave way to grass and woody bushes like tumbleweed, then taller plants, almost trees, and heavy vines, until it was hard to go on. I moved as quietly as I could, listening for people.

From behind a scrubby tree I looked into a small clearing. At first I saw nothing but sand. Then I heard a sound, then I heard it again. A voice. At the edge of the heavy growth, a few steps away, Coley and Marta were lying naked. I squatted down and watched them make love.

...

When I came to myself I moved back through the matted green, waited awhile, and called out his name.

I advanced four or five steps, like a charging animal. I stopped and shook some branches.

"Coe-lee!"

I saw him coming toward me, with his clothes on. Marta was not with him. He hugged me. We talked at the same time, the life jackets, the hanging on, the names of the dead and missing.

Marta came into the green then, moving toward us in that steady walk I would always remember, the same hardness in her face. We made our way through the tangle and moved along the shore toward the place where Angela and Pete waited. When the growth allowed us to walk abreast, Coley took her hand and she took mine and we walked together.

"Coley," I said.

"Yeah."

"I don't want to die down here."

"Neither do I."

The sun was high when we came in sight of the camp. Angela stood up and ran toward us in her socks. Marta hurried to meet her.

"I'm going to stay, though," Coley said.

"You mean forever?"

"Yes."

"What if we lose?"

"It doesn't make any difference."

"You could take her with you back to the States."

He shook his head. We stopped walking. Marta came up with Angela and Pete. She spoke to Coley and he nodded.

"They're giving up on the others," he translated for me. "We're heading out. If this is the island they think it is, there's a fishing village on the other side. It's not too far to the mainland."

"How far do we have to walk?"

He got the answer from Marta.

"Six or eight hours."

"She knows her way around pretty well," I said.

"They used to vacation here when she was a kid," he said, "if this is the place we hope it is."

It was a tough walk in the sandy soil but we all made it pretty well except for Pete. She held herself erect and lifted her feet like she was walking in deep mud. With every step her foot sank into the soil and nearly disappeared. She panted and swung her sweet potato arms.

Coley and Marta stayed close to each other. No one talked.

Marta was right about the fishing village. Ten or twelve boats pulled at their ropes and bumped against posts that were green and shiny with slime from the sea. There was a strong smell of fish. When Marta spoke to them the people offered us food and water. Three of them pulled Marta, each in a different direction, each toward his own boat, jabbering. There were a few women and some boys of maybe twelve or fifteen standing farther up the beach, staring at us.

If pride is a sin, I was sinful that day. The voices and the looks of love were following us, asking for chocolate in the streets of Paris, past fallen swastikas, through the Arc de Triomphe and on to the boat Marta led us to, a red broad-bottomed boat with two oars and three wet planks to sit on.

Sitting with Coley on the creaky seat, pulling backward and forward as he did, I felt closer to him than I had ever felt. I thought I understood what he was talking about that day when we were shooting billiards and he said, looking down his cue stick, that he wanted "to stand close to greatness."

I looked at him. I liked him. He turned to look at me as we went forward with the oars, shifted our grips and pulled back. We glanced frankly into each other's eyes and pushed forward again, grunting and sweating.

...

We came to shore among some large rock formations. The water was rough but there wasn't any trouble except that Pete had to get out and wade when the boat scraped bottom. Marta spoke to Coley, and he followed her down a road off to the left. Pete and Angela fell in behind them and I stayed close.

Nobody seemed to be worried about the loss of our guns, or about anything else, for that matter. We chatted like people on the way to church. There were no signs of soldiers or of anyone at all. I trotted a few steps to catch up with Coley. "It seems to be over around here," I said.

"Or it hasn't started yet," he countered.

The sun setting at our backs ran our shadows out before us, sliding across ruts. We had not had anything to eat or drink for hours. I had expected Pete to be dropping to the ground, asking us to wait, but I think she could have carried Coley and me both. From time to time she hummed a song I didn't recognize but wouldn't forget.

As we cleared a rise, Pete stepped to the front and extended her arms to hold us back. Across a brown scrubby field was a wooden house, charred black and smoldering but still upright. Pete moved ahead and we followed.

"Oh, my God," Coley said. Then we all saw it. The black shape of a man nailed onto the front wall by two bayonets through his chest, some of the roasted meat fallen away. I thought I was going to vomit.

We looked for a moment and then we started up again behind Pete, moving a little faster.

"Who did it?"

"I don't know."

"Ask them who did it."

"No."

After we got water from a well behind the house, Pete—still captain—led us across a ditch and into some sparse woods. I thought we were going to bed down for the night but we took a way parallel to the road and walked in single file, not speaking, taking limbs in our faces and tripping over roots, waiting whenever one of us had to step away and go to the bathroom. When it was dark we took to the road again. We walked all night. I was walking in my sleep. When the sun came up in front of us I thought it was going to take my eyes out.

We left the road again and kept walking. We passed two more burned houses. The wall of one had fallen. We could see an arm sticking out from under it, most of the meat burned away.

"Coley," I said.

"These are our people," he told me.

"I know."

"How do you know?"

"Look at Marta and Angela and Pete. Look at their faces."

"Yeah."

"We've got into something, haven't we Coley?"

"Yeah."

. . .

"Listen," he said, holding his hand up. Everyone stopped.

"It's a car," I whispered. We all fell down. My stomach was working into the earth again. A bug with black, shiny wings crawled between two blades of grass just under my nose.

When the car had passed Pete led us farther from the road into a grove of small trees. I thought of safari movies with lines of litter bearers. The last one in line always got an arrow in his back.

Nearly every house had been burned. Everybody we came upon was dead. All men. We walked five abreast across the furrows of an old field. Marta pointed to hills ahead of us.

"That's it," Coley said. "The other side of those hills is the river, the Río de Nunca Jámas. The capital is just on the other side. We've got to get across."

Pete stopped us and the women sat on the ground.

"Squeezed together beyond those hills," Coley told me, only partly in anger, I think, partly in fascination, "on this side of the river, are half the poor people of this country. It's one of the most famous slums in the world."

Coley reached down for Marta's hand and pulled her to her feet. I turned to help Angela but she was already up. Her socks were caked with blood. We made our way back to the road. A few yards ahead of me, Pete's immense buttocks contended with one another as we walked on toward something.

. . .

We stood at the foot of a hill looking across a river at the capital. We could see the slum that began with its first hovels off to the right. Everything was quiet. A few cars and a truck or two could be seen moving through the distant city streets. Smoke, maybe from a burning building, rose in a slowly spreading stalk and flattened.

"What now?" I asked Coley.

"We've got to cross the bridge."

I looked to see what he was squinting at. Shading my eyes, I could see the bridge downstream to our right. There seemed to be guards at each end of it.

Pete motioned for us to follow and turned back around the base of the last hill. As we passed one of the countless shacks, a hut barely big enough to stand up in, maybe ten feet square, she rattled her knuckles on the Coca-Cola sign that made up most of the front wall.

"Hola!" she said. "Hola!" There was a rustling inside. Thin and filthy rags that served as a curtain over the entrance split and a face appeared. I thought of the clubhouses we used to build when we were children.

Pete and the face talked for a minute and then Pete turned around and spoke to Marta. Marta spoke to Coley. He took a five out of his wallet and passed it along. A hand came out and took it. Then the face and the hand fell back and the curtain closed. Pete sent the girls in.

"Now what are we doing."

"I don't know," Coley said.

"I was just curious."

We sat on the ground near Pete and we waited.

"Coley."

"What?"

"Angela's man, you know, he threw me off the boat. He saved my life."

"Does that surprise you?"

"He nearly killed me before."

"And what do you make of that?"

I could see the dark bloodstains in the dirt where Angela had stood.

...

When the women came out they were dressed as peasants, as dirty and bedraggled as they had been, but different. The limp and washed-out skirts they wore could have been seed bags. Their heads were in scarves. Pete motioned for Coley and me to go in.

There was a kerosene lamp and the place smelled sharply of it. The corners of the little room were dark but I sensed that there were people there. The face from the doorway held out pants and shirts. We took off our jeans and sport shirts, as filthy now as anything we could exchange them for. For the first time I realized that we stank. We smelled like the whore that first night back in San Pedro. We stood there in our underclothes until the face that could have been a man's or a woman's or the devil's own let go of the trousers we were meant to put on.

Our shoes and socks were wrapped in old newspapers, packages we took with us out into the light. When we had become accustomed to the glare I saw Pete standing where we had left her. She was too big to get through the door.

"I guess she'll have to wear what she has on," I said.

"I suppose."

"What do we do if the soldiers speak to us?"

"She knows."

"Anyway," I said, "they wouldn't shoot an American. Not in cold blood."

"I guess not."

"I'll tell them I'm a journalist. I'll say I lost my papers."

"Good," Coley said. "That's a great idea. Maybe they'll let you call your paper."

More than ever I wanted to go home.

...

From somewhere across the river we heard the sound of gunfire. Coley said rifles, but I don't think he knew any more about guns than I did. I rolled the newspapers tight around my shoes and hugged them to my chest. The firing stopped.

Marta took Coley by the arm. She spoke to him in a voice so secret I was jealous.

"Coley . . . Coley . . ." she said, and then the syllables ran together in Spanish that he was coming to understand better and I could not understand at all. They walked away from the rest of us. She talked and he listened. When she stopped talking he ran a finger over her lips. They sat down under a tree that looked like it had been there for a thousand years. I joined them to get off my feet. Marta left us and she and Angela walked off somewhere.

Coley picked up a stone to turn in his fingers. He looked at it as he talked, wiping the dirt from its surface, polishing it.

"We have to get by the guards at the bridge," he said.

"So how do we do that?"

"The women will do it. Then we're going to take their uniforms. The women will be our prisoners."

"Jesus, Coley. Can't you explain it any better than that?"

"Don't worry about it. Just let it unfold and fall in with it."

"Then what?"

"I don't know."

"We're going to kill the soldiers, aren't we?"

"Not you. Not me."

"But us."

"Yes."

"I can't," I said.

"Then don't get in the way."

I thought he spoke with a Spanish accent. With a flick of his thumb he sent the pebble flying. I thought of a catapult throwing a stone across a moat, toward a raised drawbridge.

"It's going to be all right," he said. "The whole country is with us."

"Us?" I said. "I don't know who we are."

Pete called us over. She gave each of us two banged-up, rusty buckets, three with holes and one with no bottom at all, and put our shoes in a couple of them. She swatted Coley on the butt and we walked down the slope toward the water, edging over to our right to get closer to the bridge. The pebbles and pieces of broken glass and metal scrap, nails, and tin cans that lay around the hill grabbed at our feet. Before I got to the river I was leaving blood where I walked. The guards on the near end of the bridge were watching us.

"Quit walking like your feet are tender," Coley cautioned me. "They're looking at us."

"They are tender! All the skin is gone."

"Think about something else. Think about Mozart or getting it on or something. Keep your face down."

Fifty yards away, we saw Angela and Marta coming down the slope, directly toward the bridge, smiling at the guards and talking together in an animated way. At first the guards held their rifles at ready, then they let them fall, held loose by the barrels. We couldn't hear what they said, but soon both the women lifted the fronts of their skirts and giggled like children. Coley turned his eyes away toward the river but I didn't blink. One of the soldiers held a hand out like a grapefruit was in it and bounced it. The other guard put his arm around Marta's waist. She kissed him on the mouth. Then all four of them disappeared into the shadows under the bridge, into the bushes and high grass.

Coley ground his teeth. He started to say something but stopped. After a few minutes Angela appeared and waved at us and we moved slowly forward. Under the bridge we found Marta and Angela working to get the uniforms off the dead soldiers. We hurried to help, Coley with Marta and I with Angela. The open throat of our guard still poured a stream of blood when we moved him. I vomited on him, nothing but stomach juices. The buttons didn't want to pass through. Coley's guard had messed in his pants when he died. Most of it was in his underwear. Only a little was in the pants Coley had to put on.

. . .

The uniforms fit well enough except for my helmet. We decided I could carry it from my belt the way the soldiers sometimes did. When we got up on the bridge I tried to hide my scruffy beard with Angela's panties, which I held for bait, signaling the guards from the other side to come over. A sergeant came with only a little hesitation. He left the other—evidently a corporal or a private—to keep watch. I dropped from his sight before he got close enough to recognize me, or fail to recognize me. When he got under the bridge he found the women lying nearly naked on their own clothes, smiling. In ten seconds he was dead. In less than two minutes both women were dressed and Coley and I held them at gunpoint as we crossed the bridge. At the guardhouse we took the young corporal by surprise. Angela cut his throat. There was not a sound. He looked at me with startled eyes. He was sixteen or seventeen. Angela took his socks and put them on while Coley went back across the bridge and brought Pete. Coley and I, awkwardly holding two rifles each, marched all three women into the city. We saw a foot patrol and then two soldiers in a jeep. I was certain our beards would give us away. Or the extra rifles. My heart was beating so hard the guns were shaking. I tried to look sadistic. One of the soldiers in the jeep yelled something and pointed at Pete and they both laughed, but nobody stopped us.

We walked the last blocks to a church as casually as if it were Sunday morning. We were let in by a back door and led through a couple of small, dark rooms to the sanctuary. There may have been thirty people there, almost all of them men, a few women, and four or five boys and girls of fourteen or fifteen. A couple of little kids and a baby or two. Everybody seemed to be asleep, lying down in the pews or slumped over in them, trying to sit up. The stained-glass windows were all broken out, an eye here, a head there, sometimes the whole window. One of the saints had a jagged hole in his belly. Another was missing a leg. There was a hole in the front wall far above our heads. Two of the pews were splintered, like a hand grenade might have gone off under them.

Standing between the two pulpits of the split chancel, his right arm in a sling, was Flavio. Above him, hanging almost horizontal on a great black chain from the ceiling, staring down at us, was a gigantic crucifix, torn loose from its nest on the ceiling. Jesus looked like a man on a hang glider.

...

There was a quiet but almost frantic reunion. We all embraced and the names of the dead were exchanged again. Flavio and Marta hugged for a long time and then Flavio hugged Coley and me with his good arm. He kissed Pete. She picked him up and held him over her head, brought him down and kissed him on both cheeks with the great slugs of her lips. The people in the pews looked up casually. Some of them had their own slings. Lying in the aisles against the walls a few of the wounded were groaning. This seemed to be happening somewhere else. I looked down on the scene and saw myself but it was like a dream. I was up there, but I was somewhere else, watching it all.

"Why are you here?" This was Flavio, and he was suddenly angry.

"We were supposed to come," Coley reminded him.

"It is over," Flavio said.

One man had an arm cradled in the open front of his shirt. Some had bandages around their heads or their necks, made of torn clothing, all colors and dirty and bloody. A few nodded a welcome to us. Our uniforms didn't seem to stir much interest.

Flavio sat on the altar rail between Marta and Angela, facing the pews, with his good left arm around his sister. Pete stood behind the lower pulpit, leaning her elbows on it, gazing out at the congregation. Coley and I sat in the front pew to face Flavio and the women. Flavio kissed Marta on the forehead.

"What now?" I asked.

Flavio pulled Marta closer to him.

"Nothing," Flavio said. "It is lost."

"You mean everywhere?"

"Everywhere."

The girls looked at the floor. Pete stared out over the people sitting like worshipers. Coley moved to take a seat on the rail beside Marta and took her hand. I felt profoundly alone.

"We heard fighting," I said. "Gunshots, some kind of explosion. There must be something still going on."

Flavio took a slow breath and got to his feet. He stepped away from the altar rail and stood beside me. He put his free hand on my shoulder.

"There was no fighting today."

"But the shooting."

"A patrol found a group of our people hiding in a café. They shot them and blew up the building."

I was going to be killed for nothing. We shouldn't have come into the city. There was nothing to do here. I looked over the pews and around the church. I walked up and down the central aisle. On the floor under the pews I saw rifles, gun belts, knives. I sat down in the front pew and stared at the air in front of my face. I got up and sat on the back of the pew with my feet on the seat.

"Would somebody please tell me why we're in this place and what we're supposed to do here?" I didn't try to keep the anger I felt out of my voice. Actually, I was whining. I wanted to cry, and I was afraid I would.

"Take it easy," Coley said.

"You understand everything, don't you?" I blurted. "This is fine for you. This is what you wanted. Isn't it? Isn't this what you wanted? We got shot at and blown up and now we're going to die here for one . . ." I almost said *piece of twat* " . . . for nothing."

I was out of breath. I glared at Coley until Flavio spoke.

"By the time the last part of the city fell back to the government there was no way to tell you not to come. We sent a man to meet your boat but it did not arrive. I am sorry you came."

"We're not," Coley said.

"So what do we do?" I asked.

"We wait."

"For what?" I stomped my foot. "Wait for what?"

"For dark. If they do not find us here before dark some of us will get out."

"We found you," I mumbled, and kicked at the air.

"Yes."

"And we leave the city then?" I said.

"Of course."

"And then," Coley put in, "we can join forces with the others."

Flavio moved his head around like he was trying to pop cricks out of his neck. He lifted his bad arm with his good one and adjusted the sling.

"There are no others."

"In the south?" Coley said.

"Nothing," Flavio continued. "There is nothing in the south."

Coley was on his feet.

"Martinez! The army! There was a whole army."

"Nothing."

"The whole country? That's it?"

"That's it."

Coley's shoulders dropped. His hands hung loose at his sides. He grunted like he had learned that he had been calling an old movie by the wrong name. He turned away from us and walked off. Marta followed him into a small room off the sanctuary.

I looked again at the quiet faces. Even the faces of the children seemed ancient.

"I'm sorry about your uncle," I said to Flavio.

"Thank you," he said.

"Flavio?"

"Yes."

"If they come here, before it gets dark, do we fight?"

"We will have to fight."

"What if we . . ."

" . . . surrender?"

"Good soldiers have surrendered."

"They would kill us, anyway," he mumbled. "It would be worse. If they find us, we have to die here."

. . .

They found us. A banging, probably of gun butts, on the great wooden door of the church. A waking inside as if a graveyard had come suddenly alive. Grabbing for guns. Finding cover. Bracing. Coley and Marta hurried back into the sanctuary and found their rifles. They ran through a small door and reappeared in the choir loft, high above the pulpit, just level with the floating Jesus. Pete stayed where she was. Angela knelt behind the other pulpit. Flavio took a pistol from his belt, holding it in his wrong hand, and handed me a shotgun. We took positions at opposite ends of the altar rail.

I would take aim with the .410 my grandfather gave me for my eighth birthday and miss and my grandfather would say, "We gonna starve to death if we don't straighten the barrel of that gun."

I could tell that my face was drawing itself into something I might not recognize if I saw it in a mirror. I wanted to wake up. I would pretend to be dead and then I would surrender and tell them I had been held hostage.

A few feet away a boy of twelve or so knelt on the first pew with his back to the altar. His gun was resting on the back of the pew, its barrel pointing toward the ceiling. I imagined that a green shoot grew out of it and budded and bloomed into a single white rose. A red-lipped girl sitting beside him lifted the rose from the barrel of the gun and carried it to me. When I took it from her she smiled at me and the flesh fell away from her face.

Then the door gave way. Soldiers stumbled and tumbled in. They fired automatic rifles and wood and plaster flew everywhere.

They were running between the pews firing at people not a foot away from them and clubbing the fallen with the butts of their rifles. The screaming was a nightmare. Soldiers kept coming in through the wide doorway. Flavio was firing a pistol. I raised my shotgun and pulled one of the triggers. I heard somebody yell in pain above all the others but I don't know if it had anything to do with me.

Soldiers crawled over their own and ours as they moved toward the altar. Some used bodies for cover. I heard a back door fall in and looked to see two soldiers coming toward us with their guns raised. I closed my eyes and pulled the other trigger. When I looked one of the soldiers was lying face down. The other was sitting against a wall. Flavio nodded at me. Sounds of gunfire and the wailing and the calling of holy names echoed off the wood and stone around us. As I turned back toward the sanctuary I saw the twelve-year-old go down. One of his arms came off. The few of us who were left alive were falling back. Pete came down from the pulpit. Coley came down from the choir. We ran to a small hallway leading to the back exit, the one we had come in by. Coley was dragging Marta. I heard somebody crying like a child. It may have been a child, but we couldn't go back.

. . .

"Let her down," Flavio told him. "Let her go."

Coley didn't respond. He was bent over with his hands in Marta's armpits. People were running past us. The shooting had almost stopped. Pete turned Coley around and held him against a wall. Angela made the sign of the cross. Flavio closed Marta's eyes.

. . .

We moved back to the sanctuary entrance, keeping low. I held onto my empty shotgun. A few rebels behind pillars and squatting in alcoves were slowing the soldiers down a little. I knew they would die there and that we ought to stay and die, too. An old woman with a rifle and a gray shawl with fringes was shot and fell to the floor in the aisle, then she began to rise. My eyes followed her body to the top of the church, where it broke the dome of many-colored glass and continued rising until it was out of sight. The soldiers watched with mild interest as one by one, and then in groups of threes and fours, the bodies of all the dead followed her. The twelve-year-old went with the first of them and his arm followed by itself. Marta brushed against me on her way.

Flavio picked up a rifle, checked it, ran to the front pew, and started firing over the back of it. Coley followed him. I heard a cracking sound and looked up to see the head of Jesus dangling above us. It turned to face one wall and then the other. I heard shots behind us. I turned and raised my empty shotgun.

Flavio spoke in Spanish to Pete and she handed him a grenade.

"We could not do this before without killing our own people. They are dead now, anyway." He spoke as if he were mumbling to himself while he baited a hook. He pulled the pin and tossed the grenade in an easy arc into a cluster of soldiers near the front door. They tried to get out, scrambling over themselves, trampling their wounded and dead, but there was no time.

"Leave the guns," Flavio said.

. . .

We turned at the first corner and looked to see if we were being followed. I saw the clear, red tracks of Angela's torn feet tracing our way. I took her hand. Two soldiers were running toward the church but they didn't see us. Then from somewhere there was a shot and the captain fell to the street. She lay on her face with one arm underneath her body and the other reaching out. Her index finger was twitching. Angela got to her first and tried to roll her over. It took all four of us to do it.

She had been hit in the neck. Blood came out of her mouth. She coughed bubbles.

"Mama's coming," she said. "Where are you?"

Then she died.

Angela made the sign of the cross. We hid under the trucks and in alleyways. Patrols passed, sometimes with prisoners.

. . .

We came to a café. Flavio led us to the back door where we were let in.

Flavio told us to get out of our uniforms.

I had forgotten we were wearing them. The owner found trousers and shirts for us. Mine were too big around and the sleeves were short.

"If soldiers see you in the kitchen they will ask you questions," Flavio said. "Go sit down with Angela at one of the tables. It will be dark soon. She will try to lead you then to the American consul." He left without speaking again.

Angela was sitting on a kitchen chair cutting what was left of her socks off with a pair of scissors. We waited while she washed her feet and wrapped them in clean rags and put on a fresh pair of men's socks. She tried her weight on them, walking carefully at first and then almost casually out of the kitchen into the eating area, but the blood was already beginning to seep through the packing as we followed her to a table near a wall.

"I wonder if Martinez is dead," I said, half to myself. Coley didn't say anything.

"Next time it won't be Martinez, will it? It'll be Flavio."

"Flavio is Martinez," Coley said, in a flat voice.

"What do you mean?"

He shrugged and looked out the front windows. He dug with a fingernail at the scarred paint on the tabletop.

I had never been happier in my life.

"What's he going to do now?" I asked.

"He's going to start a revolution."

We ordered beer. Stuck over the bar above a dirty mirror a sign said HAMBURGO TIPO AMERICANO. In the mirror I could read backwards a large banner hanging over the front door inside the café, the sort of thing we have over the streets for rodeos. It said YANKEE GO HOME.

There were only four other people in the room. One was the bartender. No one was paying any attention to us.

    ...

       We had almost finished the beer when the front door swung open and five soldiers came in. We tried not to look at them. They stood in the middle of the room, kicked over a couple of chairs and tore down the YANKEE GO HOME sign. It floated to the floor and dropped across the table and a chair. They called for beer, and the bartender sat out five open bottles. They stood at the bar and drank them in silence. When they were finished one of them threw his bottle and shattered the mirror. The bartender didn't move and said nothing. The owner didn't come in from the kitchen.

They asked for the bartender's identification and traded the card back to him for two bottles of American whiskey. They opened one of the bottles and passed it around among themselves. Then they capped it and left, laughing at something as the door shut. We drank the rest of our beer. The bartender turned on lights that hung from the ceiling in globes that looked like plastic pumpkins.

A few more customers came in. I made rings on the table with my bottle.

I wondered what my parents were doing at that moment. They would know where we were, from Paul and Monk, or Paul's father. My mother would be sitting by the phone asking my father to call the State Department again. My father would be telling her not to worry, that everything would be all right, that the fighting was over and there wasn't very much anyway, that we're probably still in Mexico. He would think I was probably dead.

A man at one of the tables was getting loud. What he was saying or the belligerence in his voice seemed to make his friends uneasy. Angela, too.

I asked Coley.

He said he couldn't understand drunk Spanish.

Angela translated: The man had lost a son for nothing, that Martinez is dead for nothing.

As I looked at the man in what was left of the splintered mirror, he seemed to be put together of two or three different people.

"You can tell him it's not for nothing," Coley said. Angela seemed both amused and frightened that he had spoken to her in English. He repeated the words in Spanish.

"No, Colee. Está borracho."

"He's drunk," Coley translated.

"She's right," I said.

"He has a right to be drunk," Coley answered with an edge.

"Absolutely he has a right to be drunk."

Angela seemed intent on balancing her empty beer bottle on the little end but I knew she was listening to the man.

He seemed to be cursing everything. It was dark outside. A couple more people came in and gave the man a wide margin as they made their way to the bar. Angela stood up and motioned toward the door with her head.

"Vámonos."

Coley was reluctant to leave. I was not. As we passed by the man's table Coley stopped. Angela took his arm and urged him on. He took a step with her and then pulled his arm free. The man noticed us then and looked up, finally quiet.

"Colee, no!"

Coley spoke quietly. The man seemed confused, like he was having trouble focusing. He stood up. Coley offered his hand. The man stared at him and swayed.

"Colee, no!"

"Coley, come on. He doesn't want to talk to you. What can you say to him, anyway?"

Coley turned his head to face me with his hand still extended toward the man.

"I'm going to tell him that I love him."

"Coley, don't do that."

He was looking at the man again, waiting.

"If I can't do that," he said, "I can't do anything."

"Soy un amigo," he said.

The man cried out and pulled a long knife, almost a sword, from his belt. Coley was about to speak when the man lunged at him, knocking the table over, sending the other customers scurrying, some through the door.

. . .

One of the two young soldiers continued to question the few other people who had not run from the building. One came over to where I stood with Angela and looked directly into my eyes.

"American?"

I nodded. He looked at Angela. Nobody volunteered anything. I gave him our names.

"Come," the soldier said, speaking to me in English but looking at Angela.

"What about my friend?"

"What friend?"

"Let me cover him up."

The soldier threw me the banner he had torn down earlier. I folded it a couple of times and spread it over Coley's body. His feet stuck out. As we left the café I looked back to see the heavy sheet spelling O HOME from his head to the shoes that were not his.

...

The soldiers talked among themselves. We all crowded into a jeep. I thought we were going to prison to be questioned in the dungeon. One of the soldiers had a hand between Angela's legs. She didn't move or say anything.

The jeep stopped at the American consulate. I looked at the sergeant for permission.

"Well?" he said. "Get out."

I looked at Angela. Her face was a mask.

"Let her come with me," I said.

The sergeant grinned.

"Do you want to go with us or stay here?" he asked me.

I started to crawl over one of the soldiers and get out of the jeep. I turned back toward the sergeant.

"Please let her come with me."

He put his foot on my chest and pushed me onto the concrete. He yelled something at the two guards behind the iron-grilled gate and the jeep pulled away.

...

At the consulate I was asked a lot of questions by a thin man who seemed to be concentrating. He didn't seem to think my answers were very good. He finally closed his green notebook and told me to wait. The cubicle was as stark as a doctor's waiting room, with three straight chairs and a small table. I waited for almost an hour, increasingly uneasy, until a fat, bald man who said he was the deputy consul came in and told me I had a room in a hotel nearby and a ticket home, that I had been unconscionably stupid and that my father's congresswoman had called about me two or three times.

Nobody wanted to listen to anything about Angela or anyone else. Mostly they were busy and they had pretty much of an edge on toward me. I didn't blame them for that. I tried not to think about Angela. I couldn't do anything. They wouldn't listen. It wasn't their concern. She wasn't an American.

I never saw Monk again. He made it back to the university and got all his stuff and then he just disappeared. I could check back and find his family, I guess, but I won't.

I had a professor tell me once that our character shapes our choices. I'm not sure now that we make any choices. Who I am determines what I do, and then what I do determines what I become, which determines what I do. People get PhD's out of crap like that. If I still kept a journal I might write it down, but probably not. Anyway, somebody else has probably already said it. And I guess it's better that we think we make choices. Otherwise everything just stops.

...

Two days later, early in the morning, with a shave and a kind of a haircut and a change of clothes, I was on a plane headed for home by way of New Orleans. I sat by a window and watched the waves of heat rising off the blacktop. The consulate hadn't been able to recover Coley's body. I would have to go see his parents as soon as I could.

An attractive woman about my age with bright blonde hair sat next to me, in the middle seat. Next to her, on the aisle, a young woman with cinnamon skin turned through a Spanish-language fashion magazine. When we were in the air the blonde turned briefly to face me and spoke, barely moving her lips.

"I thought I was going to spend the rest of my life there. This is the first plane out in more than a month."

"I know," I said, offering my hand. "Kelvin Fletcher."

"Rebecca Martin," she said, touching my fingers just enough to see if they were warm. "That was some kind of vacation, I can tell you."

"Me too," I said. I looked at the Latin woman. She was ignoring us. She had a full, bright face. I undid my seat belt.

"What were you doing down here?" I asked her.

"My father is the American consul."

"Where are you headed?"

She undid her seat belt and smoothed her skirt.

"New Orleans. I go to Sophie Newcomb. That's a college." She said it like it was a question, raising her voice on the last word.

"I've never been to New Orleans," I said, trying to sound playful, like I was sort of joking. "Maybe you could show me around."

"I'll be pretty busy," she said. "I've missed a lot of classes."

The woman with the cinnamon skin closed her magazine and closed her eyes for a moment. When she opened them, she took a deep, slow breath. I really liked her a lot. I leaned over the consul's daughter and tried the only phrase in Spanish I could think of.

"Hola," I said softly. "Soy un amigo." Or I thought that's what I had said, what Coley had said.

The woman looked at me with confused eyes. Rebecca let out a little laugh and put a hand over her mouth.

"What's the matter?"

"What were you trying to say?"

The woman was looking at her magazine again, but I don't think she was reading it.

"I told her I was a friend."

"You said, 'Soy enemigo.' 'I'm your enemy.'"

"No. I didn't."

"Yes, you did."

. . .

"You got a bug in your glass," Rebecca said.

"No, I don't have a bug in my glass." I kept staring at the lights in the liquor. I wanted to say, I was thinking about pouring this over your head, taking you somewhere, and getting your clothes off.

"I have a toast," I said, and lifted my glass.

"What to?"

"Some friends and some enemies."

She smiled and raised her glass to mine.

I was taking the first sip when I saw the reporter from Pete's boat coming down the aisle. He moved easily, putting his hands to the backs of the seats to balance himself against the slight unevenness of the flight. He stopped beside my seat and looked at me with no expression. I thought I heard a camera click as he winked. He walked past me toward the back of the plane. By the time I could turn in my seat to see where he went, he had disappeared.

I looked out the window, half expecting to see him there, but all I saw was the luminous curvature of the earth. As the plane banked toward home, it seemed that I could see all of Latin America, then all of the western hemisphere, with a white moon above it and a curtain of stars beyond. We continued to rise until I could see the sun and the other planets, and then we continued to rise until the sun was only another star, and I saw new constellations, the galaxy, all the galaxies, and then another curvature encircled us.

Over the intercom came a crackle of Spanish. Then, in a kind of English, heavy with Spanish: *Good morning, ladies and gentlemen, this is the captain. We are flying at thirty-five thousand feet . . .*

Out the window the earth's horizon was brilliant and real. Rebecca —the consul's daughter—rested a hand over mine.

"How long," she asked, "are you going to be in New Orleans?"

ACKNOWLEDGMENTS

Thanks to the editors of *Arkansas Literary Forum, Arkansas Times, Descant, New Letters, New Orleans Review, Prairie Schooner, Red Clay Reader,* and *Shenandoah,* in which some of the stories have appeared, and a very special thanks to Jo McDougall and Steve Barnett.